THE WHITE BONES OF TRUTH

CRIS NEWPORT

Books By Cris Newport:
* Sparks Might Fly
The White Bones Of Truth

*not published by Pride

Production: THE WHITE BONES OF TRUTH
Producer: PRIDE PUBLICATIONS
Director: CRIS NEWPORT
Take: FIRST EDITION
© 1994
ISBN 1-886383-15-4

Cover art by Chris Storm.

Lyrics found in chapter five by Jennifer DiMarco.

Interior artwork and cover design by Pride Publications.

All rights reserved, including the right to reproduce this book or portions thereof in any form whatsoever, except in the case of short excerpts for use in reviews of the book.

Printed in the United States Of America.

Dedication
to M.P. who was the first inspiration
to my partner, Jennifer, who made it real

Author's Acknowledgments

I never thought this book, first begun and then abandoned in the late 1980s, would ever find its way into print, but thanks to the following people, it has. Jennifer DiMarco read the first several chapters and believed in the book even when I didn't and kept after me until I finished it. Nathan Strong, my technical advisor for the biological aspects of the book, set aside his initial disbelief in engineered humans and graciously gave of his time and expertise so that Corlay Llewellyn could be fully realized. Any errors in this area are mine alone. Rachel deThomas-Anderson and Erica Walker read a late draft of the manuscript and provided valuable feedback. Debby Holland proofread with extraordinary care. Chris Storm, an artist of rare talent and vision, worked incredibly hard to bring the characters to life. William and Beverly Newport, my parents, provided generous financial assistance so that you could hold this book in your hands. My heartfelt thanks to all of you.

THE WHITE BONES OF TRUTH

CRIS NEWPORT

CHAPTER 1
AWAKENINGS

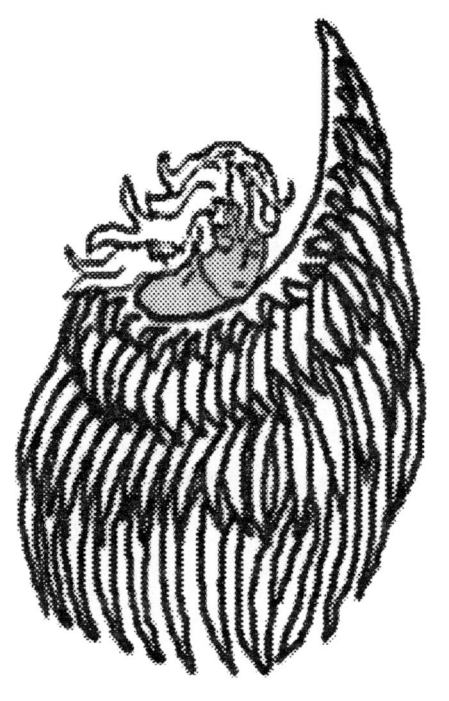

CHAPTER ONE: AWAKENINGS

You never get used to it.

Michelle David opened her eyes to semi-darkness, cursing herself for falling asleep. Through a gap in the heavy curtains, she could see the flickering lights of the city and the sky going grey with dawn. She eased herself from under the heavy arm of the sleeping client. Her bare feet made no sound on the deep pile carpet as she crossed to the bathroom. She waited until the steam had covered the mirrors before she stepped into the shower, let the hot water purify her.

There are no gods, she thought.

The client was still sleeping as she finished dressing: a soft pair of cotton pants, billowing white shirt. The clothes comforted her, felt soothing against her skin. She never felt clean anymore. Stuffing her evening gown into a carry bag, she slipped out of the room. The door clicked quietly behind her. The turbo lift took her down through the chrome and glass high rise to the building's exit which was three storeys above street level. She stepped out of the lift and walked across a brightly lit lobby toward the Tube. Sliding her pass card through the reader, she pushed the turnstile with her hip and walked through the reinforced glass hallway to the edge of the deserted Tube platform.

Beneath her feet, the city street was nearly empty. PowerCars hovered below her, waiting at an intersection for the light to change. Steam billowed from an all night noodle stand near the crosswalk; the solitary vendor dozed on a wooden stool. A few red and gold taxis cruised by, neon signs flashing prices, and a black Peacekeeper vehicle that

CRIS NEWPORT

looked more like a tank than an urban patrol car crawled along, bright white lights sweeping for and aft. It paused at the entrance to an alley almost directly below where Michelle stood and she saw the light run up and down the grimy exterior of the buildings. There was a crash as though something had fallen over or someone had run into something in an attempt to find the cover of shadows, but the 'keepers did not emerge from their protective bug-like machine.

Michelle snorted. She was not surprised. It took a serious infraction to draw the 'keepers out of their crawlers these days and when they did emerge, they were encumbered with so much hardware it was a wonder they could move at all.

Raising her eyes, Michelle saw a sliver of pink bloom along the edge of the eastern horizon, a horizon bisected by a jumble of buildings sticking up like spikes into the still dark sky. Oh rosy-fingered dawn, she thought, remembering the ancient poem. Could dawn's first touch still make things new? Bring hope? The promise of change? Michelle shook her head. There was no point tormenting herself with useless fantasies.

Circular lights embedded in the concrete at her feet began to flash, and she heard the rumbling of an approaching car. The shiny silver cylinder shot out of the tunnel, slowed at the platform. Michelle stepped inside and sank into a cushy bucket seat. She pressed a button on the armrest that would chime when the Tube reached her stop on the other side of the city, then closed her eyes. She was alone in the car. Lights from the buildings on either side of the Tube's opaque tunnel pulsed like heartbeats against the thick glass windows as the Tube raced silently along.

Seven thousand Credits. That's what he had paid for

THE WHITE BONES OF TRUTH

an evening with a Star. Seven thousand Credits. It wouldn't even begin to pay back the debt The Studio claimed she owed them. If I had only known, she thought. I never would have quit my job at the Food Warehouse. I would have refused their offers. I would have walked away.

Corlay Llewellyn picked up the photo again. Michelle David's bright blue eyes stared back at her. She slid her hand into the VR glove and swung the eyepiece into place. Her fingers twitched as she punched numbers on a telepad only she could see and then she heard the click of connection. There was a chime and a holographic image appeared before her. He was an incredibly attractive man and so obviously not real that Corlay had to laugh. "Good afternoon," the holograph said. "You have reached the central message center for The Studio. My name is Sven and it is my pleasure to assist you. Please listen carefully to the following menu for the appropriate selection. If you already know your party's access code, you may enter it now."

Sven, a created persona for The Studio's enormous computer-assisted telecommunications system, moved smoothly through the one hundred and forty options for connections. Luckily, the publicity department was within the first ten and she was spared the fifteen-minute recital.

Another computer voice answered in publicity, this one an Asian woman with a too-bright smile and fire-engine red lipstick. Corlay had to listen to twenty-three selections before the computer recited the one she needed. Finally, after being transferred a third time, Corlay heard a distinctly human voice on the other end of the line. After identifying herself and allowing The Studio to verify Corlay's identity and Credit line, the woman appeared on her screen. Like the two holographs, she was also attractive, but did not have the obvious perfection the holographs boasted. She didn't smile, nor did she make eye contact, but kept her gaze on the desktop in front of her which had several different screens all revealing data about Corlay. She asked, "Are you on line?"

It was a stupid question. Corlay could not have this conversation without it, but it had become a formality of all business transactions and she pushed her irritation down to answer, "Of course."

"Link to MBDATE." Corlay moved her fingers. A multi-colored calendar appeared before her. "See anything that suits you?" the woman asked.

"Friday." Corlay saw the date she had chosen wink out of the options.

"Your payment, please."

Corlay cleared the screen, accessed her bank account and sent the electronic transfer to The Studio Publicity Account with a tag that designated it as belonging to M. David. Corlay wondered how much, if any, of that money Michelle actually saw. The woman thanked her, gave her the information about meeting time and place, and, without ever looking up, severed the connection.

Carefully drawing off the VR glove and replacing it in its protective case, Corlay turned away from the desk to the drawing board. Pens and pencils, brushes and inks. A large watercolor drying. New artwork, illustrations. Her work. Her love. For nearly ten years she'd been a successful commercial artist, so successful, in fact that she'd retired from commercial art seven years ago at the age of twenty-eight to become a private painter for select patrons who paid well and

THE WHITE BONES OF TRUTH

on time. This allowed her the anonymity she desired and had not had in the commercial art world and a schedule that anyone in the present age would envy. No five-hour commutes on MagLev Trains, hurtling up and down the California coast at one hundred miles an hour. No standing in line for coffee, food or Credit checks. She could live inside this apartment for weeks if she had to, and sometimes she did. It was just easier that way.

The VR links kept her in touch with the few friends she had and assured her patrons she was still alive and working. But after this favor to Michelle David was repaid, it would all be over. She could finally be at peace. No more feeling like a hunted animal. No more the outcast. She would repay her debt and release Joshua's Trumpet. She would bring down the walls on a system she despised and then she could close her eyes for good.

She hoped her body would cooperate when the time came. But she was not certain that she would be able to maintain her female resting gender, even though she practiced her biofeedback techniques daily, throughout what was sure to be an emotional evening. But Michelle David had seen it before — the transformation. It had not frightened her then. Perhaps it would not frighten her now.

Lifting her ID Card from where she'd left it on the table, Corlay stared at the picture. She read the typed information on the card. Name, address, identification number. Red capital "A". Androgyne. Genetic Experiment. Outcast.

Corlay put the card away.

Michelle could not hold back her tears. She turned her head away, brushing ineffectually at them with well-manicured hands. "I'm sorry," she murmured. Her friend, Saundra, took Michelle's hand. She had no words of comfort for Michelle and was momentarily ashamed at the relief she felt knowing she was too old to be of use to The Studio any longer. Saundra knew she would live out her days here, in the furnished beach house that had been her retirement gift from The Studio. Looking at her friend, Saundra wished she could have convinced Michelle of the truth long ago. But even if she had, would Michelle have listened? The young ones were so hungry and by the time they were satiated, the damage was done.

Michelle was so beautiful. Unblemished skin, deep blue eyes, a wide generous mouth. Discovered at a booth at a VR Convention in Los Angeles, helping her then-boyfriend, Jack, sell some useless accessory that had been all the rage for about four months. Her body browned by the sun, innocently seductive in faded jeans and a white tailored shirt belonging to the boyfriend. Michelle had told her the story a hundred times.

"I feel like those women at the old dance halls, you know?" Michelle said quietly. "With their little dance cards that are always full. I'm tired all the time."

Saundra stroked Michelle's hand in silence — the skin warm to her touch — felt the fragile bones underneath and imagined the blood running through her veins. "Would that we'd been born ugly," she said.

Michelle looked up at her swiftly. "Once I thought it was all worth it," she said. "I would have given anything to be on the screen. Now I wish I'd listened. To your advice. To Jack's."

THE WHITE BONES OF TRUTH

"Let it go, Michelle," Saundra insisted. "You can't undo the past." The light from the window cut across Michelle's face, softening the hard line of her high cheekbones, dripping down her long sun-browned neck into darkness between her breasts. Saundra stared at the dark hollow at the base of her throat, imagining kisses there, remembering her own years of turning her head away from the hot seeking mouths and feeling as if she were two people in bed with a stranger. One floating near the ceiling, rehearsing lines for the next day's shoot, a mind cut off from feeling. And the other a body below a stranger's, unresponsive at the core, moving with the rhythm of coupling without needing to participate in the dance.

"Did you ever like it?" Michelle asked.

"There were times..." Saundra began slowly, but didn't finish. Then after a long silence she added, "But it was all the same."

"I don't know which is worse, the women or the men."

"There are more men."

"Men make more money."

"It's always been that way." Saundra looked toward the open window, lifted her chin to feel the incoming breeze. Twilight was creeping inward from the corners of the room. "I'm not much comfort to you, am I?"

"You're fine." Michelle drew her hand away slowly. She drank the last of her coffee and rose. They parted in silence. Saundra, wrestling with her solitary regrets, watched Michelle drift into the fading light.

Outside, feet on the cool sand, Michelle felt, for a moment, a sense of peace. There was still this, she thought, looking at the pale sand and white-capped water. There was

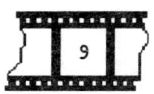

still the cooling breeze and the evening stars. Buried deep inside her lay a hope that she could change this life. Flight perhaps. Underground.

The small computerized watch on her wrist beeped, reminding her that in three hours she had to meet a new client at the beach house The Studio rented for these occasions. The cook, she imagined, would already be there, chopping fresh vegetables on an oak board. Steamed rice. Broiled fish. There were benefits to this life. Glittering moments like wine sparkling in a crystal glass.

Her clean clothes were in an overnight bag. Casual. That's what this one wanted. Simple. She spoke into her watch, asked for a MagLev Car to pick her up at the nearby Rail Intersection. Settling her bag on her shoulder, she turned away from the sea.

At the beach house, Michelle showered and drew on a loose pair of cotton slacks and a raw silk turquoise blouse that accentuated the indigo blueness of her eyes. No makeup or jewelry. She brushed her golden hair in long smooth strokes, losing herself in the rhythm of this simple movement, the tingling feeling running along her scalp. At exactly seven p.m. the door chime sounded. Michelle rose from the dressing table and went to greet the stranger at the door.

Corlay stood on the stoop, smoothing her hair absently. When the door swung open, Corlay lifted her head and there was a sudden shock of recognition that brought tears into her eyes. She felt as though she was in the midst of a waking dream. Everything blurred as Michelle cocked her head, as if searching her memory for the face.

"Do I know you?" Michelle asked. Her voice was like water over smooth stones.

"We met once, years ago. But I don't think you would

THE WHITE BONES OF TRUTH

remember me. I'm Corlay Llewellyn."

"The painter?"

Corlay nodded and Michelle said, "You look familiar, but I can't place you." She stepped aside to let Corlay pass and added, "A number of my ... some people I know own your work. It's really wonderful."

"Thank you," Corlay said softly.

Michelle led Corlay into the living room and through the open french doors to the deck beyond. They stood at the rail staring into the distance. A pale sliver of moon hung near the waterline. "You can see Jupiter and Venus tonight," Corlay said, pointing. Michelle came close and Corlay could smell the scent of her skin like a sharp knife cutting through the dense, sea-drenched air.

Her nearness was intoxicating. And dangerous. Corlay moved away a little, and catching Michelle's puzzled expression from the corner of her eye, smiled, thinking of her innocent beauty and its high price. She felt her genetically altered senses expanding like fog billowing from a singular source that rolled to encompass them both. Michelle's mood and all the emotional turmoil that bubbled below the placid surface were suddenly clear — a swirl of bright colors denoting sensation and feeling.

And as Corlay was being immersed in a textured pool of the complexities that made Michelle unique, Michelle studied Corlay, feeling puzzled by the smooth skin and strong features. Corlay, slightly taller than herself, moved with a jaguar-like grace. Michelle noted the slender long-fingered hands, brown as the wood they rested on, let her eyes travel up the corded muscular arms to the broad square shoulders. Corlay's hair spilled onto her shoulders, streaked from the sun in blonds and golds and ambers. When Corlay turned to

smile at her, there was gentleness in her black eyes and small smile lines around her soft full mouth.

A servant brought wine. Corlay poured two glasses; their fingers brushed and as they did, Corlay's senses heightened. She felt the tingling awareness of Michelle's interest, curiosity and a sadness deep at the core. They drank in silence facing each other. Corlay rested quietly in that silence, radiating calm. Images moved in her mind and she knew that a painting was emerging. She closed her eyes, sank into the colors.

"Is something wrong?" Michelle's voice slid into her ears.

"There are colors here," Corlay murmured. "Gold and red. Something that lies hidden, like bones beneath the skin."

Michelle felt a knife thrust of fear pierce her. "How could you know that?" she asked.

"What?"

"What lies hidden."

Corlay's black eyes opened. "It's not that kind of knowing," she said. "I feel it."

Michelle felt the hairs on her arms raise up and something like static electricity seemed to crackle in the air for an instant, then was gone. Michelle relaxed. You're too tense, she admonished. Reading into everything. She mentally shook herself and changed the subject. "Would you like to eat now?"

"I would, thanks."

Candlelight bounced off the crystal, smoothed the polished wood surface of the table. Corlay ate slowly, savoring each flavor, commenting with pleasure. Michelle felt calm. Safe. That was something she hadn't felt in a long time. And as her guard came down, she allowed herself to wonder

THE WHITE BONES OF TRUTH

what the feel of Corlay's hands would be like. Tonight she would not regret what she must do. She actually found herself looking forward to it.

After the meal, they returned again to the deck. A servant brought coffee laced with chocolate. The moon set, seemed to slide into the water and rest beneath the surface. In the stillness between the breaking waves, Michelle was aware of the quiet, the sound her own breath made moving in and out of her body, the quiet breathing of the stranger beside her. The soft scrape of the mug against the wood railing. The sound of fabric sliding across fabric. A foghorn sounded far out to sea, and waves pushed against the shore with slow persistence.

"You are a gracious hostess," Corlay said, reclining in a deck chair, stretching long legs hidden beneath dark smooth cloth out before her.

Michelle could not find the words to tell Corlay how she felt at this moment. "If all my life could be this simple," she whispered.

Corlay smiled. "Yes," she agreed.

"Are you very successful?"

"I'm content with my work, and people don't seem to mind paying outrageously for it." Corlay laughed. "At least I have a talent that supports me."

"And you're free," Michelle said before she could stop herself.

"Free? Are any of us free anymore?"

Michelle felt relief flood her, grateful Corlay was content to speak in the abstract. "No. Not really."

Corlay smiled sadly then looked away. Pain rose like a tight fist in her chest. Michelle came to the chair and sat down. The feel of Michelle's thigh against Corlay's leg made

Corlay ache, her fingers against Corlay's cheek spoke of a soothing warmth. Corlay wrapped her fingers around the back of Michelle's neck and held them there without force, enjoying the softness under her fingertips.

Corlay had not forgotten what she had paid for, but was nonetheless surprised when Michelle leaned forward and kissed her cheek. For an instant, Corlay lost herself in the delicate exquisite sensation of another's mouth against her skin, then she pulled away. This was not why she had come here.

But Michelle did not seem to notice. Now her body was full against Corlay's and her fingers were at the buttons of Corlay's shirt. No, Corlay tried to say, but no sound emerged. She tried to push Michelle away before she felt the hormonal surge, felt the tightening of her muscles while confusion melted into desire. She tried to take a deep breath, tried to still her mind, but she was overwhelmed by panic. She had not chosen this. She did not want this. She cried out in a way that was unmistakably not a cry of pleasure. Michelle pulled away, startled. "What—?"

In the shaft of light that spilled out across the deck, Michelle watched Corlay close her eyes as tears leaked out. She noted how tight the muscles were beneath Corlay's clothing, the way her voice had deepened, the unmistakable bulge at her crotch, and the pieces of a puzzle she didn't even know she'd been working out clicked together. "You're an androgyne," Michelle said in a voice without repulsion. She felt Corlay's exhaled breath brush across her cheek.

"Yes. Didn't The Studio tell you? Don't they usually tell you when ... but I was not planning on ... I had not thought you would want to touch me. I was not ...."

Michelle struggled to make sense of what Corlay was

saying while trying to recall the information she'd read on the ride down here. There had been no mention of Corlay's gender — or official lack thereof — but that didn't surprise her. The Studio sometimes conveniently forgot such details. Pushing those thoughts aside, she concentrated on Corlay. "Can you do that at will?" she asked. "Shift like that?"

"Yes. I can control it. But sometimes if I'm aroused or startled, it just happens." Corlay opened her eyes again. "I'm also an empath." Then she added dryly, "It's a kind of added attraction. I sensed you generally prefer men and my body began to compensate, to mold itself to your desires. I'm sorry. I should have been paying more attention. I was sensing your emotional colors, so to speak, and not paying attention to your physical body."

Michelle laughed. A hearty genuine laugh.

Corlay flushed. "I'm sorry. I didn't mean—"

"—No. It's perfect. You have no idea how wonderful it is to hear that you saw something other than my body." She reached out and took Corlay's hand. "Tell me more," she said.

After a moment, Corlay drew breath and continued. "My resting gender is female. I was born female. But I'm also male. I can sense things about other people, most androgynes can. Some are telepathic or telekinetic, I'm an empath. I felt that perhaps you would be happier if I were male. That it would please you."

"Please me?"

"You must know in order for me to be here I have paid my fee. And it is more than rumor which fuels talk of Contracts."

Michelle pulled back. "I can't discuss—"

Corlay waved her hand. "Please. Don't misunderstand

me. Those of us with the money to pay for evenings such as these have heard talk of the contractual, shall we say, 'obligation' you're under. I had hoped to give you an evening's respite from those demands, Michelle. It was never my intent to force you to touch me." Corlay paused. "It must be repulsive for you." Her eyes touched Michelle's face. "To touch me."

"No." Again the caress, like a warm breath. "You're beautiful."

"Don't feel obligated to spare my feelings. I won't give you a bad report."

"I meant it." Michelle rose and went toward the light. "Come inside."

Corlay followed her into the light, past the now empty table gleaming silently, and into the bedroom at the other end of the house. Corlay watched her move across the room in the darkness, switch on a dim light near the bed. She returned to press herself against Corlay. "Will you stay?" she asked.

"It would be difficult," Corlay whispered.

"You don't repulse me."

Corlay's dark eyes were like fire on Michelle's skin. Michelle lifted her own shirt over her head, took Corlay's hand and laid it on her breast. She felt the hand tremble. "Will you just give in to it?" Michelle leaned close and whispered. Her hands strayed to Corlay's waist, the button on her dress pants. "Feel the clean lines of desire, Corlay."

Corlay groaned and let go of the tight reign she was keeping on her form. She let Michelle's desire, or at least the projection of it, wash over her like water. She felt the hormonal rush like fire in her veins, felt desire like flame. She felt Michelle's hand tug again at the pants. "Come here," she

THE WHITE BONES OF TRUTH

said, leading Corlay toward the wide bed.

As Michelle began undressing, Corlay watched with a growing unease. This was not why she had come here. When Michelle called her to the bed, Corlay obeyed, sitting down beside Michelle, her eyes moving along Michelle's body like a slow caress. She traced her fingers across Michelle's skin. Her hands eased along Michelle's muscles, down her arms and legs, rubbed her delicately sculptured feet.

Corlay turned Michelle over slowly and put her hand on Michelle's back. "Relax," she murmured, her fingers raising goosebumps. Then she laid both hands against Michelle's shoulders and began to ease the day's tension out of them. She worked slowly down Michelle's back, focusing on steadying her breathing, relaxing again into an unaroused state. By the time she had reached Michelle's feet, Corlay had shifted completely back into her female form and stilled a mind that had raced with fantasy. This was how she wanted to repay this debt. With kindness and gentleness. With an evening's peace instead of an evening given to sexual favors, no matter how much Corlay desired it, no matter how much she had longed to be under Michelle's hands and mouth all those years, all those dark nights. No. The debt had to be repaid in kind. She had survived thirty-five years on her own imagination and even this much, even this touch was more than she had hoped for, meant more than she could say.

She felt Michelle struggling to stay awake, heard her voice mumble, "Corlay."

"Hush. Rest. Let me please you."

And if Michelle thought she would feel Corlay's hands slide to her breasts or slip between her thighs, she only felt Corlay's fingers probe her aching muscles and tension flowed away from her, seemed to leak through her fingertips and

onto the floor. Her mind was full of brilliant colors that swirled and danced. As sleep cradled her, the colors muted, faded into a still, aching blueness.

Corlay touched Michelle's shoulder blades, ran her fingertips against their fine edges encased in soft skin. She thought of wings. Sun-warmed golden feathers. Corlay kissed the smooth plane of skin between them. "Sleep well, little angel," she murmured as she covered Michelle with a blanket, turned off the light and headed for home.

Back in the city, at the ragged edge of sleep, Corlay dreamed. She was lying on a dirty floor in a place that smelled of rotten vegetables and human sweat. Her adolescent body was racked with pain, dots swam before her eyes. Her muscles tensed and released of their own accord. She was in the middle of a seizure and flopped around on the floor like a beached fish. Faces pressed towards her. Spit from an onlooker ran down her cheek.

She screamed and the sound woke her.

Corlay pressed the heels of her hands into her eyes, felt tears leak out. She shook her head to clear it, pushed back the tangled sweat-soaked sheets and stripped off her clothes. Naked, she padded silently to the shower stall, ducked into the water before it was fully warm. The cold shock raised bumps on her skin and she shook her head, flinging the water from her eyes.

After two mugs of dark coffee, a luxury few could afford, she began to feel more like herself again. The dream was no more than a fading fragment of memory. At her easel, she began painting a woman with wings.

❉ ❉ ❉

Jennifer Jonston, JayJay to her friends, stuck her arms into the front bib of her overalls and cocked her head toward the speaker in the control room of Sounds By Gene. Gene, a gangly ex-pro rollerblader whose body was tending to fat, slumped down in the only comfortable chair with his eyes closed. JayJay looked at him, thinking that his eyelids were the only place on his body not covered with coarse black hair.

She pushed her straight earth-colored hair away from her face with both hands then tucked them back into her overalls, under her large breasts, so that they rested against her round belly.

"You look like you're playing with yourself when you do that."

"Fuck off, Danny-o," she said, not turning to look at her lead guitarist who was slouched with practiced indifference against the back wall. As the song ended, he pushed off and sauntered over to her, his bare feet splayed out in front of him. He looked, she imagined, like a nag that needed to be put out to pasture: swaybacked and skinny with a hard round belly that came from too much liquor and not enough food. He lit another cigarette and let it dangle from his lips in what he believed to be a seductive gesture. JayJay found it simply silly.

"Well?" Gene said, his eyelids slid open slowly to reveal bloodshot faded blue eyes.

JayJay looked over at Danny-o. He squinted at her through the smoky haze of his own making and shrugged. Her eyes moved past him to Kay, their lead singer. She was the youngest member of the group, barely post-pubescent. Small and slight with a heart-shaped face and lanky dirty blond hair that fell to her shoulders, she was totally unremarkable without her performance makeup on. She was gazing down the front of her scoop neck tee-shirt as if willing her breasts to grow and nodded without looking up.

Alejandro picked up his fretless bass from where it had been lying on the floor, his raven black hair falling like wings over his face. Like Gene's, his eyes were bloodshot, but his were red from exhaustion instead of too much Drug. His chiseled face was softened only by the two-day growth of beard he hadn't found the time to shave off. It made him look dangerous and unpredictable.

"I think it's fine," Alejandro said, his words slurred by his accent and tiredness. "Can I go home now?"

JayJay shrugged. "I don't see why not. Rehearsal tomorrow? Eleven?"

Everyone nodded. JayJay, the band's leader, lingered in the studio. Alejandro poked his head back in. "You coming home?" he asked.

"I'll take the Tube. See you in bed."

He nodded and shut the door behind him.

Gene rose slowly from the chair as if he wasn't sure where his body left off and the rest of the world began. Despite his heavy dependence on Drug, he was, in JayJay's opinion, the best damned engineer in the business. It was through his influence they'd snagged this opportunity to submit a tape to Oilslick Records, and JayJay, though she hated to admit it, knew she owed him one. And knowing Gene, he'd ask her to take it out in trade.

"We need another session in here to finish this song. Plus there's a new song I want to lay down tracks for sometime next week. Can you book us for a couple of days?"

"Sure," Gene slurred. His hand groped along the top of the console, searching for the battered computer pad that served as the studio's date book. "Just fill it in."

THE WHITE BONES OF TRUTH

JayJay selected the days she wanted. By the time she was finished, Gene was already taking hits off his three-foot bong and the room was filled with the sickly sweet odor of the burning herb that JayJay hated. She didn't bother to say goodbye because she knew he wouldn't remember it one way or the other.

※ ※ ※

The next morning, everyone looked reasonably well-rested. The dark circles under Alejandro's eyes had almost disappeared, and even Kay seemed in a half-decent mood.

JayJay sauntered into the large warehouse space they used for practice five storeys above street level on the rougher side of town and took a disk from the pocket of her overalls. "I've got this new song..." she began but was drowned out by groans before she finished. "No. Wait. You're going to like this."

"No more Smasher. That stuff sucks," Danny-o pronounced.

"No. This guy's been dead for about fifty years."

"Oh, great. Zombie rock," Danny-o griped.

Ignoring him, JayJay went to the player and inserted the disk. She punched a few buttons and the room exploded with sound: saxophone, drums, hand claps, guitars and over all soared a sweet male voice that seemed to know no limits.

"Who's this guy?" Alejandro asked, his face alive with curiosity.

"His name was Jon Anderson. Was real big back in the latter part of last century. He was with this band called..." she dug into the pocket of her overalls and produced a crumpled piece of paper. "*Yes.*"

"Yes, what?" Kay asked.

JayJay just stared at her. "The name of the band was *Yes.*"

"Oh," Kay chewed her gum and looked out the window as if practicing her bored stare.

"Listen," JayJay pressed on, appealing to Alejandro directly now as he was the only one who seemed the least bit interested. She knew Danny-o was secretly, but for him to admit it was like getting him to admit that he might not be the superior being the Society Reformers were always telling him he was. Although she was fond of Danny-o, sometimes his steadfast adherence to the bullshit of male superiority made her crazy. He only tolerated her, JayJay suspected, because she was his ticket out of the marginalized ghetto existence they were all subjected to, and when they performed, she deferred to both him and Alejandro. At least in public. But in private, in these rehearsals, it was another story. Here she was in charge, and everyone knew it. She hated the dichotomy, the lies, the pretending that everything was fine when, in fact, almost everything sucked just so they would at least have a chance to make it. Hard choices. She drew breath and continued, "I think this song will give us the name we've been looking for for the band: State of Independence."

Silence. JayJay looked at the band. Although both Danny-o and Kay seemed disinterested, JayJay knew it was a survival tactic. Neither of them would have lasted long if they hadn't mastered the indifferent stare. But Danny-o, she could tell, was angry and Kay had paled. She didn't like to take unnecessary risks and JayJay, on some level, couldn't blame her. Kay and Danny-o both owed a lot to JayJay. Her vision and persistence had given them first a place to sleep and the guarantee of at least one decent meal a day. Later, when the band became more successful, they'd each had some pocket

money. And now, when "Night Tube" was in heavy rotation on WKMA radio, they were closer than ever to achieving their dream — a Contract with a big label. Marginalized pseudo-political bands were very hot right now, but JayJay, in spite of her desire for success, was leery of the inevitable next step: mainstream music. She wanted to push the limits of what they could do and say now and was willing to take more risks than the others.

"That stupid idea could get us killed," Danny-o hissed. "Hell, we're lucky the Peacekeepers aren't already on our asses. With a name like that we'll be in solitary so fast our heads'll spin."

Kay looked from Danny-o to JayJay as if not sure whose side she should take. She said nothing. Alejandro, JayJay's lover of six years, just looked at her and smiled a little half-smile. He shrugged. He generally went along with what she wanted to do, but she couldn't read him now.

JayJay collapsed heavily onto the two mattresses that served as a couch. Two storeys below them the Tube rumbled by. "You people are all a bunch of chicken shits."

Alejandro unfolded his lanky, well-muscled frame from his perch on the window sill and said, "Why do you want to do this?"

"Because I'm angry. Because we have rights."

"We have no rights," Danny-o reminded her. "That word doesn't even exist in the 'keepers' vocabulary. Besides, civil disobedience went out with the twentieth-century. Get with the fucking program, JayJay."

"I thought the purpose of this band was to make a political statement. I thought that's why we decided to do it," JayJay persisted.

"That's why *you* decided to do it," Danny-o

corrected. "I'm just in this for the incredible cash rewards." He laughed mirthlessly.

"Look, JayJay, it's not that we don't like your idea," Alejandro put in, "It's just that maybe we should think about the timing of this. Maybe changing the band's name isn't the best idea right now. At least until after Festival. Or we get an offer from Oilslick."

"No, you're wrong. That's exactly why we should do it now. Festival's less than a month away—"

"—Three weeks from Friday. Yesterday," Kay put in, looking at her fingernails.

"Yeah. Thanks. Anyway," JayJay continued, "Festival would be the perfect time to announce a new name."

"No," Danny-o said. "That name sucks. No new name, JayJay."

"Think about it before you shoot your mouth off, Danny-o," JayJay shot back.

"I don't have to think about it. I'm telling you that we're not changing the band's name. Alejandro, back me up on this, will you?"

Alejandro looked uncomfortable. "Let's think about it, okay?" he said, trying to pacify everyone. "We can talk about it again later." Danny-o sighed with exaggerated patience and bent to pick up his guitar from the floor.

"Fuck you all," JayJay said. She pushed herself up awkwardly from the couch and snatched the disk from the player. The room was plunged into silence. Plopping herself behind the battered drum kit she yelled, "Well, come on, assholes, are we going to practice or not?"

CHAPTER 2
FLICKERS
IN THE DARK

CHAPTER TWO: FLICKERS IN THE DARK

Michelle awoke the next morning in the house by the ocean. She hadn't meant to sleep all night. She had to be back in Screen City by eight a.m. As it was, she was going to be at least an hour late. But as she rose from the bed, it didn't seem to matter. For the first time in weeks she felt rested, relaxed. The last thing she remembered about the night before was a kiss between her shoulder blades. She called The Studio. Lying to the secretary was easy — Corlay had stayed all night, worn her out, in fact. That, she knew, would please the execs and in turn, they would calm down her already overly nervous director until she arrived.

She called for a MagLev Car and walked out to the Rail Station where the Car would pick her up. She hated travelling in Cars. Like the old style subways but a hundred times more efficient, the Cars ran on a magnetic track suspended seven feet in the air. Once Cars merged onto the main track, speed was regulated by computer, and no one could change lanes by jumping from track to track. Pick up and departure exits were programmed from the time of call and could not be changed, either. A passenger had only to sit back and relax while the Car whizzed along at speeds that sometimes topped one hundred fifty miles per hour.

Michelle hated them because they were regulated by machine and were, she felt, even more prone to error than if they'd been driven by humans. A large power surge or failure could cause catastrophic results. But that had only happened once, when the Cars were still in what the designers liked to call their "infant" stage. It had been an expensive infancy,

claiming more than five hundred lives in several horrible accidents before all the design flaws were resolved.

But MagLev Cars provided accessible and rapid transport and for no other reason than she'd make it to the studio before 3:00 p.m., Michelle had pushed aside her reservations in favor of convenience.

She slipped into the dirty white car and pulled the hatch down until it clicked into place. Pressing the green "ready" button, she sat back in the plush bucket seat and held her breath until she was on the main track. Then her mind wandered. The passing scenery was first spacious beach front property, then a series of small units crammed together and finally the heavily industrial grey and silver buildings that stretched all the way down the coast to Screen City.

She felt herself lulled by the electric hum of the Car, and turning on the radio, found a station that wasn't blasting Societal Reformer peace-love-freedom bullshit every minute. She didn't buy it for one second. The new California government was just as corrupt and definitely more unjust than the old one had been. Women's rights were all but eroded, and a return to what had once been known as "family values" had been adopted nearly a half-century ago. Those comfortable phrases were nothing but smokescreens for the male power bonding that had evolved like an out-of-control virus. A return to the roles men and women had played in the middle of the last century. Peace. Love. Freedom. They were just words now. Words without meaning. Words out of context. It wasn't about freedom. It was about a serious lack of choices.

She closed her eyes as the announcer came on to say, "And now something from our local favorite, The Bandshees, with their hit single, *Night Tube*. Rumor has it that they're

THE WHITE BONES OF TRUTH

about to sign a major Contract with Oilslick Records and something new and exciting is due out from them in the very near future. Stay tuned to WKMA, All-Hit Radio."

The song that followed the announcer's shouting into the microphone caught Michelle's attention. She stared at the radio. The drums kicked in with the chorus and Michelle felt a shiver run down her spine as she listened to the words.

You slip away
Take the Night Tube home
He pays your way
Take the Night Tube home
You've got nothing to say
Take the Night Tube home
We see you on the screen
Your life flickers then it's gone
And the power guys say
We own you from
Now
On...

When the chorus came around again, Michelle reached for a computer pad and a stylus from her bag and wrote down the name of the song and the band. She wanted to know more about them.

When the door to Corlay's apartment clicked open late the following night, she rose from her chair in the darkened screening room and took a wooden bat imbedded with metal spikes from its hanging place on the wall.

Fighting for calm, she shifted into male shape, felt her loose clothing tighten around her muscles as she tensed with

fear.

The intruder padded softly up the entryway, then called out. "Corlay? Corlay, you home?"

Corlay set down the bat and turned on the light. Her son Phoenix blinked in the harsh light, put his arm up to shield his eyes. "Did I scare you? I'm sorry. I should have called first."

"It's all right." She came forward, still in man shape, to embrace her only child, now a man himself. "Are you hungry?"

"Starved." Phoenix laughed. "As usual."

Corlay gestured to the kitchen. "I'll be there in a minute." She went back into the screening room, hesitated. Michelle's image filled the large screen. The film had just come to the love scene and the hero was peeling back Michelle's clothes while she arched away in faked ecstasy. Corlay's hands trembled slightly, remembering the feel of Michelle's skin last night. Phoenix, watching from the doorway, said nothing as Corlay turned off the film.

But in the kitchen, he said, "You really have a thing for her."

Corlay nodded.

"How come? I thought you were against the whole industry."

"I don't like most aspects of it, but my interest in Michelle David is personal." Corlay looked across the table. Phoenix's hair was coming loose from its pony-tail, falling like burnished gold around his face. When Corlay was in man shape, they looked so much alike it was almost frightening.

"I'm sorry. I didn't mean to pry. It's just that ever since I was a kid you've watched those films again and again. If I didn't know you better, I'd say you were obsessed."

"Good thing you know me," Corlay tried to joke. It didn't work and they both knew it.

"Are you in love with her or something?"

"I think it falls into the 'or something' category." Corlay went to the food storage unit. "Chinese okay?" she asked.

"Sure."

Corlay took out several boxes and popped them into a microwave unit mounted on the wall. As she relaxed, she felt herself shift back into her resting form as the adrenalin rush subsided. "Remember how I told you when I was an adolescent I had violent seizures?"

Phoenix nodded.

"I had one of them in the Scan 'n' Save Food Warehouse near Screen City. I was waiting in line with just a few things. I hadn't been feeling well and wanted to get home. It happened so suddenly. One minute I was standing and the next I was thrashing on the floor like a fish on a ship's deck." Corlay's voice fell into silence as she remembered. The microwave beeped, breaking into her thoughts. She shook herself and brought the boxes to the table. Handing Phoenix a pair of chopsticks and taking a pair for herself, she poked at the mixed vegetables and rice that steamed in the thin plastic box. "The girl at the register pushed the onlookers away, took me to the back room and let me lie down. She stayed with me." Corlay looked at her son and said, "There are so few people who will even touch an androgyne, an act of kindness is like an act of God." Corlay paused, then said, "I never forgot her. I never thought I'd see her again. You can imagine my surprise when I saw her in a film a few years later. I guess she'd been discovered by some talent scout."

"The girl at the register was Michelle David?"

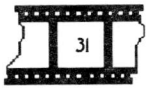

Corlay nodded.

"Now it makes sense. Why didn't you tell me?"

"It wasn't a memory that had much to do with you, I guess. And for a long time I didn't want to talk about it. But it's not so hard now. A lot of time has passed and most people probably don't even remember I'm an androgyne. It's not like there are many of us left and they certainly didn't make more."

"I'm glad they made you."

Corlay squeezed his hand. "Thanks. I'm glad I had you. And that I was able to repay Michelle David for that act of kindness."

Phoenix looked up, his eyes full of questions.

"You've heard about the Contracts that The Studio offers aspiring actors?"

"I've heard rumor," he said and his eyes slid away from her. Corlay noticed, but let it go.

"It's not rumor, Phoenix. A few days ago I spent seven thousand Credits to spend the night with Michelle David."

"You what? You bought another person?"

"No." Corlay shook her head. "I paid for her time. We had dinner. We talked. I came home. I bought her an evening's reprieve, Phoenix, to repay the debt."

Phoenix didn't say anything for a long time. Then he asked, "So now what?"

Corlay shrugged, "Now I am free of that responsibility and can think of other things."

"I need to tell you something," he said, his voice almost a whisper.

For one horrible moment, Corlay was afraid he would tell her he had signed one of those damned Contracts, but he

THE WHITE BONES OF TRUTH

said, "I was arrested."

Corlay's first thought was not for his future employment opportunities — which could be severely limited to suddenly nonexistent for anyone with so much as a traffic violation — but for his safety. She wondered if she'd done the right thing in raising him to be an independent thinker, a man who was still willing to question authority in a time when even an innocent act of defiance could cost a life. "When? Why?"

"A few days ago. I got released this morning. It was a protest at Screen City against Contracts. I saw Michelle David there. She wasn't protesting, but she was watching." Phoenix's eyes were bright with the fires of revolution.

"How many were there?"

"About fifty. A small group. It wasn't just about film, it was about art and books and music. People want their freedom back, Corlay."

"Were there other Stars there?"

Phoenix nodded. "Yes." He hesitated then said, "You remember Robert?"

"Rafael's son?"

"He signed a Contract five years ago, right after Rafael's death."

"Oh, no," Corlay groaned.

"Now he wants out, but The Studio claims he owes them ten thousand Credits from expenses incurred on his last two films. He never saw a single Credit in payment from either one, but The Studio claims that his food and rent bills are too high for his B.O.P."

"B.O.P.?"

"Box Office Potential. He doesn't draw in enough yet to pay back what they claim he owes."

Corlay leaned forward. "So you know how this works. The Contracts."

He nodded. "Yeah. Robert told me everything. When they 'discover' you, they offer you a Contract. You agree to make a certain number of films over a designated period of time for The Studio. They'll take care of all your expenses. Whatever you earn over your expenses is yours to keep. But the thing is, you never earn over expenses. They set it up that way. It looks legit up front, but once you're in ... well, they won't let you break Contract until you pay up. If you can get someone to pay the debt for you, you're free. But you'll never work in the industry again." He poked at the cooling vegetables and ate for a moment in silence.

"All his life, the only thing Robert wanted to be was a Star. He dreamed himself into movies since he was old enough to hold the remote. And now ..." Phoenix spread his hands. "He f.inds out his dream is really a nightmare." Phoenix looked hard at Corlay. "It's not *fair* , dammit. Those politicos, the Societal Reformers, take everything from us — our dreams, our creativity, our freedom."

"Initially, people thought the Societal Reformers were a good thing," Corlay reminded him gently."We thought we wanted the kind of change they claimed they could make happen. Equal opportunity. The end of the Welfare State...."

"But it didn't work, did it?" Phoenix shot back.

"No," Corlay agreed. "It didn't. In the end they resorted to the status quo, to the ultra-conservative societal structure that puts men above women, whites above people of color. They've reverted to the so-called normalcy of the last century's 1950s when everything was confined to strict gender and societal codes. Then it was just adopted practice;

THE WHITE BONES OF TRUTH

now it's law."

"But if the people rebelled," Phoenix persisted. "Look at the civil rights movement. The rise of gay power in the early twenty-first century."

Corlay nodded. "But the pendulum always swings back, son."

He grinned. "Yes, it does. If history teaches anything, it's that human beings cannot tolerate oppression for long. The time is ripe for revolution. It's like a tsunami rising a hundred miles out to sea. By the time it reaches the coast, it's a solid wall of water."

Corlay did not miss the meaning behind his words.

"So there you are," he said, coming back to his original topic. "You owe all this money to The Studio. Most of the people who get suckered into these things are 'discovered' in some hole near Screen City and aren't well connected, never mind legally aware of what's happening to them. They're hungry and The Studio knows that. They'll do anything to see themselves up on that screen, you know? And if they want to keep getting the good parts, the ones with the most B.O.P., they have to do what The Studio tells them. Which, as you must have figured out, includes prostitution. The good parts go to the ones who play the game. Who will fuck the rich clients and keep the money coming in."

Phoenix stabbed his chopsticks into the nearly empty box and left them there. The extra weight made the box fall over onto the table and a dribble of sauce leaked out. "It's not right, Corlay. They never get to see any of that money."

"Even though it's tagged for them?" Corlay said, thinking suddenly of Michelle and the fee she'd paid several nights ago.

Phoenix nodded. "Yeah. Didn't you know that?"

Corlay's mind was racing. "Well, I suspected, but I didn't know," she hedged.

"But you bought into it."

"Phoenix," she snapped, her voice tight, "please try and understand this. I suspected that something like this was happening and when I called for a reservation, some of my suspicions were confirmed. When I got close to the heart of the matter with Michelle, she panicked. But over the course of the evening, certain things became clear to me. I was repaying a debt, Phoenix, and trying to give back in the only way I could."

"I'm sorry," he said. "I do understand. I'm not mad at you. I'm mad at the system."

"You should be. It's wrong."

"We can change it."

"But we're not ... Phoenix, sometimes change has to come from the inside as well as from the outside. If the Stars don't want to sell themselves, then they don't have to sign the Contract. They choose."

"It's not that simple," he insisted.

"But on some level, Phoenix, it is." She rose from the table and threw the boxes into the trash compactor. "Look, I'm not saying don't do this. You know that I'll support you no matter what. And I'll bail you out if necessary. But you also have to insist that these people take responsibility for their own actions and choices. You can't change them if they don't want to change."

"And if they do?"

"Viva la Revolution!" Corlay shouted, fist in the air and laughed. "So," she said after a moment, "how does the arrest affect your work status?"

"I'm on The List now."

THE WHITE BONES OF TRUTH

"That's the price for protests."

Phoenix nodded. "I'm driving a truck for the big trucking company downtown. Did you know that it's independently owned? That a lot of its employees are Active?"

"'Active?'"

"They're on The List for one reason or another. The foreman doesn't care what your political history is as long as you do your job. In fact, he's probably on The List himself."

"Why do you say that?"

"Oh, just some of the things he says. He doesn't have much tolerance for the government's bullshit."

"He should be careful or they'll shut him down."

"He's careful, Corlay. Don't worry about me."

"I always worry. It's a parent's job to worry."

Phoenix laughed. "So you've said." They rose from the table together. Phoenix went off to sleep in his old room. He lay on the narrow bed that seemed too small for him now and stared at the familiar ceiling. He wished he could spend more time here, but between working for Gabriel Bell downtown and the growing demand on his time from the political group Bell had connected both him and Robert with, he had little time to himself. He had wanted to tell Corlay more about his work, but had stopped himself. It still bothered him, despite her explanation, that she was so caught up with an image of Michelle David. That she had given The Studio money and bought into the entire repulsive elitist practice.

He flamed briefly with anger and then reason with all its cold logic overtook him. He saw other images on the ceiling, had other memories. Childhood memories he hadn't thought about in years. Corlay's desire for him to have a "normal" childhood, finding the Whitsons, a heterosexual couple who had posed as Phoenix's real parents at school and social events. How her eyes had tried to hide the deep hurt she felt watching him pack his belongings to spend time with his other family. How much she had given up for him. And how deep her loneliness had been.

He had never known her to have friends, really, although there had been a few people during his childhood who had been companions to Corlay. But eventually they all drifted away. And Corlay was left with her movies and her art. She seemed content, and yet he could sense a place deep inside her that was hollow. It was a place she couldn't fill herself, a piece of herself that could only be complete with another. But because she was an androgyne she did not allow herself to contemplate it. Phoenix didn't understand that exactly, but he respected it. She wouldn't talk of her early life, and tonight's story was like another puzzle piece he had to fit into place.

Sighing, he turned over. Corlay always told him he was impatient, and then she'd laugh. Where did she get such patience, he wondered. And from what depths did she draw the strength to go on?

In the screening room, Corlay chose her favorite of Michelle's films. It was the most erotic, the most revealing. And this time as she watched, Corlay recognized expressions, nuances she'd seen last night. She reveled in it, and let herself fall wholly into the netherworld of flickering lights and shadows where she could play the lover's part in the way she hadn't been able to the other night. She willed herself into the story — was suddenly there — and it was like NetSurfing. She was embodied, yet curiously disconnected from the

THE WHITE BONES OF TRUTH

physical form that was reclined on the couch. Her imagination carried her through dialogue she knew by heart and when it came time for the kiss, she could almost feel Michelle's mouth open to hers. But then the film was over and Corlay, no longer in the magical world, lay on the couch in the dim light, letting tears slide from her cheeks onto the pillow below her head.

❈ ❈ ❈

The 'keepers broke down the door to Corlay's home near dawn.

Corlay, who had fallen asleep in front of the screen, jerked awake when the solid hardwood splintered and crashed open. At first, she thought it was she they were after, a random roundup of the remaining androgynes, which still happened every once in a while. But an instant later she realized it was Phoenix they wanted.

The new grey light of morning was pressing against the windows and Corlay was barely on her feet before she was shoved against the wall by a burly man dressed in a dust grey uniform. His face was hidden behind a smoked plastic helmet and his voice was distorted by the imbedded microphone. "Corlay Llewellyn?"

"Yes. Listen, I will cooperate. Please, I'm an artist. Don't destroy —" He cut her off with an abrupt motion of his hand. She thought of the painting she'd just started yesterday and felt anger boiling up inside her. She stalled them, hoping Phoenix was awake, hoping he remembered the false wall.

"Stand out of the way."

Corlay went into her studio, began to stack paintings in a corner, in the hopes that they would not tear this room apart. She thought of all the films she had so carefully collected stacked and labeled in the closet off the screening room and imagined them in loops and circles all over her floor. She thought of her small and inexpensive possessions. She cried in anticipation of what they might do to her art. But most of all she shook and forced back sobs for Phoenix. If he was still here, he was as good as dead.

She could hear the sound of breaking glass in the other room, of knives ripping open furniture, of bookshelves being overturned, of film cans crashing to the floor.

She heard the door to Phoenix's room bang open. The sound of booted feet echoed through the hall. The same man came into her studio. "You are harboring the criminal Phoenix Whitson."

"No."

"You're lying." He reached up and backhanded her across the jaw.

In her rage, Corlay's form shifted. In her rage, she struck back and knocked the unsuspecting Peacekeeper to the ground. A moment later she was unconscious, lying amid broken tubes of paint, shattered glass and thousands of dollars worth of ruined paintings.

❄ ❄ ❄

Michelle was lying to the secretary again.

"Yes, she left something at the beach house."

"We'll send it to her."

"It's very personal. I'd feel better if you just gave me her address. I'll send it to her."

The secretary looked at her from under half-closed eyelids that were painted a bright shade of vermillion. Her

THE WHITE BONES OF TRUTH

aqua hair was spiked and teased away from her scalp, making her look more like one of the extras in the studio's recent flop "Mutant Sex On Mars" than the most highly paid secretary in the entire organization.

She sighed heavily and turned away from Michelle to tap a few keys on her computer. The printer wheezed and gasped and a small computer chip slid out. As Michelle reached for it, the secretary warned, "You owe me."

"Fine." Michelle took the chip and hurried out of the office.

All day yesterday she hadn't been able to get Corlay out of her mind, trying to place her, unable to remember. Last night, near dawn, she'd awakened suddenly out of a sound sleep with a tight ring of fear around her chest.

By seven-thirty she was at the studio, pestering the secretary for Corlay's address. She had a day off before shooting resumed the next morning. There were questions she wanted to ask Corlay, answers she needed to know.

But when she stepped off the lift into the hallway of Corlay's apartment, the hairs on the back of her neck rose and she knew something was wrong. She took her StunGun from her handbag and held it out in front of her. She came to the kicked-in door and her breath caught in her throat.

Stepping over glass and trash, she worked her way cautiously back through the apartment. To her left was the kitchen, its shelves empty now of dishware and dry goods. Further down the entryway a large room opened up on the right. She looked in. The room, decorated in reds and golds, had a large viewing screen on the wall opposite the entrance. A slit open couch lay on its back in the center of the room. Film tins littered the burgundy carpeting and the film itself was strewn like flat spaghetti all over the floor.

Two doorways opened out of this room, both bedrooms. One door had been kicked off its hinges, the other was still partially attached. Michelle went into both rooms but found no one. The bathroom on the left was almost as large as the bedrooms, with white and black tiles and sparkling chrome.

The last room at the end of the wide hallway was Corlay's studio. Huge windows and a skylight made the room harsh with light. Corlay lay amid the wreckage of her craft. Her face, bruised and swollen, lay in a small pool of blood that had leaked from her slack mouth.

Michelle ran to the still form, bent quickly and pressed her fingers to the other's throat. She felt Corlay's heart beating slow and steady beneath her cool skin. Michelle put her StunGun away and went back to the bathroom for a wet cloth. As she dabbed at the ugly gash on Corlay's forehead, she felt anger rise inside her. Who would do such a thing? she wondered although she already suspected it had something to do with the 'keepers. Did it concern the fact that Corlay was an androgyne? Had it been, instead of a 'keeper raid, an act of violence against a tiny but despised minority?

She touched Corlay's cool, smooth skin thinking again that she had seldom seen a more handsome face. Although Corlay was unusually pale at the moment, her mahogany-colored skin and the fine bone lines made her striking enough that Michelle was sure she'd turn heads in the street. She remembered the other night and the feeling of Corlay so close, the scent of her skin, the broad shoulders and tapered hands. She hadn't felt this drawn to anyone in a long time. And yet she wasn't sure whether it was physical or emotional, wasn't sure whether she would want Corlay in female form the way she'd wanted her the other night.

THE WHITE BONES OF TRUTH

Corlay's eyes fluttered open then. She pulled away even before it seemed she had registered her surroundings, drawing her legs up toward her chest and lifting her arms protectively. "Corlay," Michelle said quietly. "It's all right now."

Corlay looked at her, first in surprise then in disbelief. "What are you doing here?"

Michelle hesitated, then said, "I wanted to see you again."

"But why?"

"Truth?" Michelle asked. When Corlay nodded, she said, "Because I liked how I felt with you the other night. How you made me feel. I thought we might ... you might ..." she faltered. "I wanted to see if you felt the same way and whether you would like to spend some time with me. Be my friend."

"I have no friends," Corlay said sharply. "And I don't need your pity."

Michelle pulled back as if she'd been slapped. "This isn't about pity. I don't do anything out of pity because it's a waste of time. And being around people who hate themselves is a waste of time as well." She rose from the floor. "I'm sorry to have—"

"—Wait." Corlay held up her hand. "Please forgive me. I'm not myself right now. I think over the years I've forgotten that some people are honorable. I'm not used to decency."

Michelle nodded. "Nor am I. That's why when I saw it in you the other night, I didn't want to let it go. I had to see you again. To make sure I hadn't made it up by wanting it to be so."

"You didn't imagine it, Michelle," Corlay said rising

slowly from the floor. Michelle held out a hand to steady her. "Thanks. I have always known you to be kind."

Michelle gave her a puzzled look, but when Corlay didn't elaborate, she didn't press. "Who did this?" she asked instead.

"'Keepers," Corlay said. "They were looking for my son, Phoenix."

"You have a son?"

Corlay nodded. "Don't look so surprised. Miracles happen everyday." She laughed, then sobered. "He's become politically active lately and I think they want to scare him, try and shut him up."

"Did they find him?"

"I hope not. I don't think so. There's a false wall in his bedroom. But I was knocked out pretty early on." Corlay moved past her and into the hallway. Michelle followed Corlay out of the studio and through the other rooms, watching the tension gather between Corlay's shoulder blades as she came upon each new invasion of her privacy and each new example of the wanton destruction of her property. But when she got to the screening room and saw the films strewn all over the floor, she collapsed among the reels of film and cried.

Michelle knelt beside her. Corlay curled in on herself, pulling some of the film into her lap, sitting crosslegged and bending so far over that her forehead almost touched the floor. Michelle hesitated, afraid to touch Corlay, wanting to. While her mind debated, her fingers lifted a loop of film. What she saw stopped her cold. She looked at Corlay again, a hundred more questions blooming within her. Finally, she let her hand come to rest gently on Corlay's shoulder. Corlay did not respond, but she didn't pull away either.

Finally Corlay raised her head. She met Michelle's eyes and found them full of questions. "Are all these ... of me?" Michelle asked.

Corlay looked around the room. Again the nod.

"I don't understand," Michelle said at last. Fear was beginning to fill her. Perhaps she had misjudged Corlay. What if she were nothing more than an obsessed and wealthy fan and the other night a prelude to something more dark and dangerous? She swallowed and started to rise, but Corlay's fingers closed around her wrist in a firm grip.

"Please." Corlay's voice was soft. "I would never hurt you. Please. Don't run away." She let go of Michelle's wrist suddenly as if surprised to find herself holding it. "Let me explain something and then, if you think I'm just a fucked-up fan, you never have to see me again."

There was something in Corlay's expression that made Michelle hesitate enough to nod. She settled herself more comfortably on the floor and looked into the night-dark eyes that were cloudy with memory. "You used to work at a supermarket," she began. "Just outside the city."

"Yeah. Scan 'n' Save. A food warehouse. How did you know that?" Michelle's suspicions rose again and her voice took on a sharp edge.

"I used to shop there. When I was an adolescent, I had a seizure there. In your line. You let me lie down in the back room."

Memory flooded back, filling in the missing pieces of her fragmented recollection. "I felt I'd seen you before, but I couldn't remember the exact circumstances. I remember now," she said softly. "You looked a lot different then, like you hadn't grown into your body yet."

"I hadn't. And my body hadn't quite decided what it

was going to become. Adolescence, with its hormone surges and conflicting desires is difficult enough for someone with an identifiable gender. For an androgyne, it's worse."

"I can't imagine," Michelle said. "Mine was traumatic enough and pretty normal in the grand scheme of things. But I do remember this now that you've reminded me. It caused quite a stir."

It had been a damp and rainy afternoon. The warehouse lights seemed unnatural and harsh against the muted greys from outside. Corlay had been waiting in the checkout line at Michelle's register. She'd noticed Corlay because Corlay seemed to be in a lot of pain, her face was pale as a corpse's under the lights. Just as she reached the register, Corlay had fallen to the floor, spluttering, her face bloodless, her arms rigid at her sides. Michelle remembered running around the edge of the register, pushing people back. Corlay's bones, beneath the clear youthful skin, seemed made of clay and as she thrashed, the muscles in her arms and legs bunched and released, splitting open seams and popping buttons.

While Michelle yelled for the manager and tried to keep people back, the crowd pressed closer, their faces looming like vultures, their voices shouting obscenities: Mutant! Freak!

Michelle remembered cradling Corlay's head in her lap, caressing her cheek and talking to her, trying to get her to wake up. It had felt like a bad dream. She had never seen an androgyne before, but had heard of them, had read about their adolescent seizures.

Michelle had tried to shield Corlay's body with her own as onlookers spat and kicked. By the time the manager arrived and cleared people back, her side was aching from the

sharp blow of a boot and spit was running down her face. When Corlay came to consciousness again, she had been moved into the manager's office and covered with a blanket. Michelle had watched her dark eyes flutter open, touch her face in horror, turn away.

"It's all right," Michelle had said.

"What happened?"

"You fell."

"What did you see?"

"It's all right. You're safe here. The manager said I could take you home when you felt well enough to go."

"What did you see?" Corlay had demanded.

Michelle hadn't replied.

"Bet you've never seen anything like that before." Corlay's voice had been bitter and challenging.

"No."

"And it disgusted you."

"No." Michelle had reached out and taken Corlay's hand only to have her snatch it away again. "It wasn't disgusting. I was worried you'd hurt yourself. Do you want to tell me your name?"

"No."

The manager had come in with an icepack for Michelle. She'd been aware of Corlay's eyes on her, of the shocked expression on Corlay's face when she'd seen the purple bruise on her side. When the manager had gone, Corlay said, "That was meant for me."

Michelle nodded.

"Why did you do it?"

"Because you're a human being, just like me. I don't care if you're an androgyne or a whatever. I just couldn't stand there and let people hurt you."

Corlay's throat had worked against tears. "I'm sorry."

"It's not your fault. People are ignorant and frightened of what they don't understand."

Corlay had turned away and covered her face with her hands. Michelle reached out and touched her shoulder. "It's all right now," she said helplessly, not knowing what else to do. But that only seemed to make Corlay more upset, so she withdrew her hand slowly and sat in silence, feeling the burning ache from the boot kick flame in her side.

She had never known Corlay's name, but remembered her face, remembered the haunted expression in her eyes when she snuck out the back door of the warehouse and disappeared into the rain.

"You were like a live wire," Michelle said. "One minute crying, the next filled with rage. I wanted to do something to help you. To make it all right."

"There was nothing that could have made it all right, but you made it better. I never forgot you. During all the years that followed, I thought of you, wondered what happened to you. I went back once, to look for you, but you were gone. And then I saw you on the big screen. Part of me was glad — I hoped that you'd gotten something that you'd wanted. But part of me grieved because I figured I'd never see you again.

"When I started making a lot of money for my artwork, doors I didn't even know existed began opening. Everyone wanted a piece of it, you know?"

Michelle nodded. She did.

"And then I heard about this ... thing ... this way you could pay money to spend an evening with your favorite film Star. It's billed as a way to raise money for the next project, but anyone with enough money to do it knows that's a bunch

of bull. It's like an open secret. The promo says one thing, but the truth is different. And when I heard that, I started to hurt inside for you. Because the one person who'd been kind to me now ..."

"Was being sold like a piece of property."

"Yes." Corlay looked up into Michelle's face. "The other night, when you took me into the bedroom, I knew."

"Knew what?"

"That my suspicions were true."

"But you were wrong."

"What do you mean?"

Michelle was quiet for a minute as she tried to gather her thoughts. "You were right about what The Contract requires. We are 'encouraged' to give the clients what they want, and of course, that usually includes sex. You were right that my life is more about prostitution than about acting. But you were wrong about the other night. I wanted you, Corlay. It wasn't that you were a client. I wanted you to touch me."

Corlay flushed and stammered, "You don't have to spare my feelings."

"What makes you think I am?" Michelle countered, angry now.

"No one wants to touch an androgyne."

"I did."

Corlay looked startled. Michelle's fingertips touched her cheek and she was flooded with two sets of emotions — Michelle's and her own. When Michelle's breath brushed her cheek and then her lips grazed Corlay's lightly, Corlay felt a surge of something she couldn't identify. It felt like fire. Then she knew it as longing, desire. It was everything she'd seen flickering across the screen. But this was real and it was happening now and she kissed back, her mouth opening with

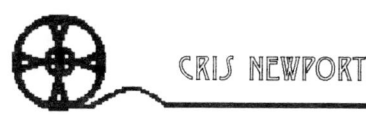

a groan. And then suddenly it was terrifying and she pulled away.

"Did I hurt you?" Michelle asked. "I..."

"No," Corlay shook her head. "No." She looked at Michelle. "I can't. I'm ..." She laughed hollowly. "... afraid."

"All right," she whispered.

There was a dense silence. Corlay took a deep breath and let it out. "Do you understand now? I could be with you through the films. I could pretend."

Michelle nodded. "You must have other friends," she offered.

"Most of the androgynes are dead. They were my friends. The ones who understood me. I know a lot of people, but there are few I trust." She let the looped film slip through her fingers. "I'm afraid it's all ruined."

"I'm not so sure. Let me make a few calls. In the meantime, I want you to come stay with me until things settle down again. I don't want you to stay here alone."

"You've done enough," Corlay said.

"I won't take no for an answer. If you won't, I'll have to insist on staying here with you."

Corlay smiled for the first time all day.

❆ ❆ ❆

After waiting for the building's carpenter to put up new doors and the locksmith to install new locks on them, Corlay packed a few things in a soft shoulder bag and accompanied Michelle to her apartment in the heart of the city.

Like most contemporary Screen City dwellers, neither of the two owned a personal transportation vehicle.

THE WHITE BONES OF TRUTH

The Tube effectively networked all of the densely populated central areas with above ground transportation. The old subway tunnels had been abandoned after an earthquake at the end of the last century had damaged most of them beyond the point of fiscally responsible repair. It had been cheaper in the long run to build the suspended track and easier to police.

The cars were equipped with surveillance cameras, but additionally, Tube police constantly patrolled the cars. Gang warfare was nonexistent now thanks to enforced curfews which had only recently been lifted and the new government's hard line position on urban violence. Although it hadn't done much else good as far as Corlay was concerned, the destruction of the gangs had been something she'd supported without question.

The lights at the edge of the Tube's platform pulsed to announce the arrival of the train. A sleek bright yellow car shot into the station, slowed with an audible whir. The doors slid open and passengers streamed out. Corlay and Michelle entered and took two seats by the door.

As the train picked up speed again for the long run between this station and the next, Corlay's eyes strayed first to the video ad displays which ran along the edge of the car's wall just above the passengers' heads. The cheaper ones merely displayed words with some generic graphics, but many were like Net terminals — full color, wide screen. Some even had a row of selection panels on the bottom edge where prospective buyers could scan for more information about a certain product or service.

Against the forward bulkhead was the familiar square news panel. Tuned twenty-four hours a day to a government-owned broadcasting company, this feature had been one of the selling points of these new machines. No more wasting time or newsprint. Now the news would be brought to you during those times when most people merely stared out windows or at each other. Cellular phones, because they interfered with the operational signals of the trains, were not allowed, and the government knew that to sell people on Tube transport they would have to come up with something that would at least attempt to build a bridge between the relative isolation of the Tube transport and the endless information and connections available outside.

So they created the news panels. Instantaneous local, national and world news, stock prices, entertainment and industry information, even a classified ad section. The only problem, as far as Corlay was concerned, was that the station was owned by the government and therefore what was broadcast was so distinctly biased that it was almost useless unless one wanted to know the current political platforms of the elected officials.

Corlay remembered reading Orwell's *1984* years ago, and nothing reminded her more of the government's attempt to control the thinking of its citizens than these seemingly innocuous boxes. She hated them and the rigid, conservative government they represented and now turned her eyes from the too handsome newscaster who was updating any interested passengers on the current number of women who were electing to give up their jobs in order to stay home and raise children, to return to "traditional values." It turned her stomach to think about the ways in which childrearing had once again become the end-all and be-all of a woman's life. How her reproductive organs were really all she had to offer to humankind. Grateful that the sound on this terminal wasn't turned way up, she looked out the smoked windows at the ragged skyline instead.

THE WHITE BONES OF TRUTH

The sky was beginning to darken and all across the city, lights were coming on. This time of day had always been Corlay's favorite. The darkening sky and the twinkling lights had made her think that somehow the city was magical, even though she knew better. Huge neon billboards flashed against the indigo sky, many now with movable pieces that formed arms or heads or even simulated a moving car. Sometimes Corlay felt as though she were living inside a giant circus tent where a hundred performers competed for her attention.

Screen City was never dark. The warm nights stretched into another seamless dawn. Neon burned against the velvet sky, Tubes glided between stations and above it all the needle-like spire of the Screen City Towers punctured the night. Music leaked out of clubs five storeys below the Tube platforms and there was laughter and liquor and back-room deals. Opening night parties with red carpets and free champagne. But underneath the glitter, there was something darker, like the fragile bones beneath a heavy-handed makeup job intended to make anyone over forty look twenty years younger. There was a sinister presence, a tension. There was frustration about the way discussions of equality were turned into sermons about superiority. There was anger about the lack of privacy and the slow erosion of the very idea of free speech.

And Corlay felt all of it, bubbling like a cauldron, felt it seeping out from the other riders. She knew that it wouldn't take much to ignite a flame from all this kindling and wondered just how soon the city might find itself engulfed again.

Struggling to distance herself from the overwhelming emotions of the other passengers left Corlay exhausted, and she was grateful that their station was approaching.

Descending the platform stairs into the cooling night, Corlay breathed deeply the scent of urban streets. Hot tar and sweat. Concrete and steel. She had never wanted to live anywhere else, but wished her city could be more forgiving, more open to difference and change.

Michelle's apartment had three bedrooms, one serving primarily as a study which formed a crescent around the main living area that was open on the other side to a breathtaking view of the city. Tall windows, free of grime, made the lights seem as if they were actually in the room. Seven storeys below, the Tube rumbled by and when she looked down, Corlay could see the yellow headlights and blue taillights of passing PowerCars on the street below. Between the buildings, in the far distance, was the MagLev track that led up the coast. On the twelfth floor, the city was silent and mysterious. Hushed by the reinforced glass and recirculated air, it seemed like nothing so much as a dream of light painted on a smooth velvety canvas.

Corlay turned from the window and Michelle handed her an oversized brandy snifter. She swilled the liquor around, watched the copper-colored liquid cascade down the smooth wall of glass. She took a sip, let the fumes roll off her tongue, up and out her nose. She joined Michelle on the couch.

Michelle turned off the light and the city sprang into an even more brilliant show of light and dark. "Can I ask you something?"

"Of course."

"The other night I felt as if you looked right through my facade on the porch, right through my skin. I've never known anyone that could make me feel so comfortable so quickly, so easily. How can you do that?"

THE WHITE BONES OF TRUTH

"That's part of who I am. I can see things. A lot of things I'd rather not see, to tell you the truth. People trust me. That's a big part of the reason I've made it as a painter, as an independent business person in a time when everyone works for The Studio or some other conglomerate. I could sell you swampland in the southern region and you'd believe it would sprout gold."

"How?"

"I sense things, what people want to hear. I could feel your sadness the other night, your frustration. But you were curious, too. About me, about where you'd seen me before. I didn't pay my money to take you to bed, but to thank you."

"What would you say if I told you I wanted you to take me to bed now?"

Corlay flushed. "I would have to tell you my deepest, darkest secret."

Michelle looked up at her, tried to read her expression in the night-black eyes. "Tell me," she said.

Corlay looked down at her hands, looked at Michelle's. "I've never been with anyone. Never made love."

Michelle's brows knitted together in confusion. "What? How is that possible?"

"Like I said, no one wants to touch an androgyne."

"That's not true. Besides, I didn't mean that. I meant Phoenix."

"Oh." Corlay seemed relieved to have the focus shifted away from herself. "Phoenix is truly a one-parent child. It's a long story. An unusual story. Are you sure you want to hear it?"

Michelle nodded. She moved closer to Corlay on the couch. "Can I sit near you like this?"

Corlay nodded. "I'd like that." She extended her hand

to Michelle and the woman took it and held it gently. They sat there for a while, quietly sipping the brandy and staring at the panorama of lights.

Michelle shifted and asked, "Would you feel comfortable holding me?"

Corlay changed her position on the couch, opening her arms and legs. Michelle moved into their protective circle. She leaned her head back against Corlay's chest. For a moment, they rested there. Corlay pressed her face into Michelle's hair, smelled the lingering scent of soap, the more musky particular scent of Michelle's own body. She let Michelle's hair trail through her fingers, thinking she had never felt anything so silky or soft, except maybe for Phoenix's baby hair. There was nothing, she admitted, that could compare to that.

And Michelle, safe for one of the first times in her life in the arms of someone who had not paid for her affections, turned her head slightly so she could hear the steady rhythm of Corlay's heart and feel it beating against her cheek. Corlay smelled of old turpentine and paint, a smell that lingered long after it had been washed away. It was embedded in her, as deep as the seventh layer of skin. She felt herself relax as she had the other night, felt her worries running out of her like water and pooling unnoticed on the floor.

"When I was nineteen," Corlay began, "I was offered an enormous amount of money to participate in a study of androgynes. It was legit. I was broke. I'd been arrested several times just for being a 'genetic mutant' and, as you probably know, was having no luck finding work.

"The people conducting the study wanted to find out if androgynes could essentially self-impregnate and carry a child to term. At first they weren't interested in whether the

THE WHITE BONES OF TRUTH

child was 'normal' in terms of physical, genetic or mental deficiencies — as they defined them — but just whether the fertilized egg would take and grow.

"There were twenty of us. Ten were self-fertilized in the first group. They took eggs and sperm from me, created life in a test-tube and implanted it. Out of the ten, three took right away. I was one of them. The other seven miscarried. But later, five out of those seven became pregnant. The other two participants were declared sterile.

"The second group was fertilized with sperm from 'normal' male donors. There was a lot of controversy then about whether or not androgynes were sterile. All ten took and had healthy children.

"In my group, of the eight of us who were eventually successfully impregnated, only three had children that would grow up. The other five children were severely retarded. Their level of intelligence couldn't even be measured. We're talking serious, serious inbreeding." Corlay paused and laughed bitterly, sending vibrations down Michelle's spine.

"Phoenix and the others were real miracles. They tried this experiment several more times but have never had as good a result. I guess it was a fluke. Maybe something to do with age or hormone balance. I haven't a clue.

"But we were paid a lot of money for a continued study that lasted until Phoenix was twenty. Our identities are kept secret for obvious reasons. As far as the Organization knows, I have no children. Phoenix has paper parents, a regular mom and pop and a different last name, but he's mine. Truly mine.

"You know, the scariest thing about this whole deal is that if they'd found twenty androgynes that could self-reproduce, I don't have any doubt they would have wiped us

all off the face of the earth. I'm surprised sometimes that I'm still alive. I really am."

Michelle shifted herself so that she could look into Corlay's face. "I want to meet him."

"I hope someday you will." Corlay took a deep breath and let it out. "I know he's still alive, but I wish I knew where he was."

"How will he contact you?"

"We have a system. But I don't know when I'll hear from him. I'll just have to take it on faith that he's okay and he'll reach me when he can."

"I don't know if I could do that," Michelle admitted. "I think I'd worry myself sick."

"It's always been this way for us," Corlay said. Then she yawned. "I think I should try to sleep."

"Do you want to sleep alone tonight?" Michelle asked tentatively.

"If I have a choice, I'd rather sleep with you."

"You have a choice."

In the bedroom, between crisp cotton sheets, Corlay fell almost immediately asleep. Michelle lay awake for a long time, listening to Corlay's quiet breathing, thinking of Corlay's whispered confession that she'd never even shared a bed just before she dropped from waking to dreaming, and dreading the next day and the nights to come when she would have to give herself again to the faceless men and women that paid to be part of her life, if only for a few hours.

CHAPTER 3
FROG IN THE WELL

CHAPTER THREE: FROG IN THE WELL

When Phoenix heard the door being forced open, he was already awake. Half dressed, he pulled on his shoes and grabbed a shirt and heavy sweater. He could hear Corlay's voice in the hallway, knew he had only seconds to make an escape.

Opposite the foot of his bed, there was a hidden panel. Installed just before the failed coup, this apartment and others in the building had once been headquarters to some of the central political figures of the time. Built as an escape route as well as a way to connect with other buildings through underground tunnels, the apartments with secret panels had been preserved and passed on through an intricate network to people who would not only keep the secret safe, but also continue the tradition of resistance.

Phoenix quickly released the spring which let the panel swing outward and stepped onto a narrow ledge. Bending nearly double, he pulled the panel shut behind him then paused for a moment to finish dressing silently. He didn't hear any noise from the other side of the wall. Then he sat on the platform's edge and put his legs on the top of a metal slide attached to the ledge that was his only route to safety. He prayed to whatever Gods existed the 'keepers wouldn't kill Corlay. He chided himself as he moved automatically. His desire to see her, the one person in his life who had always believed in him, stood by him, had overwhelmed his sense of safety — both hers and his. But he vowed, even as he swung himself into the opening, that if anything happened to Corlay, he'd personally rip the face off the 'keeper who'd hurt her.

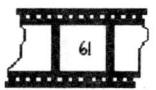

Phoenix took a deep breath and pushed off. There was no way to slow himself down once he'd gained momentum without tearing the skin from his hands. The chute was enclosed, smelled of dead air and something rotting, like cabbage or rats. In the total darkness, he zig-zagged left and right as the chute twisted and turned and felt his heart pounding in his chest. He wished he'd remembered a pocketlight.

It seemed like an eternity before he saw a pinprick of light far away. As he shot closer, the light source grew, became the open end of the chute. He tried to slow himself by digging the heals of his rubber-soled shoes into the metal but when the chute emptied him onto a pile of mattresses on a brick platform about five feet wide, he was travelling fast enough to knock the breath from his lungs.

After a few minutes of gasping and blinking into the light, he got up slowly and looked up and down the platform. About a hundred yards away, there was another chute which also opened onto the platform and another pile of rags. Corlay had told him these abandoned subway tunnels had stairways and exits, but most had been sealed shut. He tried to remember what she'd said about the closest exit but it had been so long ago and he'd never had occasion to use the tunnels, although Corlay had once, years ago. He began to walk toward a stairwell at the platform's far end, figuring he'd just have to look around until he found an open exit. And hope no one on the 'keeper's force had been too diligent about pursuing the rumor that some of the tunnel exits were still open.

When he got to the exit on this platform, he found it had been bricked over. With a curse of frustration, Phoenix walked back to the middle of the platform. He stared down

THE WHITE BONES OF TRUTH

the tunnel. This was probably his best bet. He turned and looked the other way. It didn't make much difference, he thought, which way he went. So, turning in his original direction, he climbed down a short ladder and stood in the middle of the tracks. They stretched out in front of him, gleaming a little in the dim platform light. He began to walk.

❊ ❊ ❊

They used to close the set for love scenes, the ones in which both parties were totally nude and writhing around together on a bed surrounded not by the filtered moonlight the audience would see, but rather by several tons of equipment and more than one pair of staring eyes. They used to allow the personal dressers on the set during those scenes to rush in with oversized robes for the between-take conversations. They used to do a lot of things to make the stars more comfortable that just weren't done anymore.

But today, Michelle David, who had the highest B.O.P. of any woman in the business this month, was not in the mood to be stared at. The few hours she'd spent with Corlay had changed her, crystallized something inside her she hadn't known existed.

She was tired of the long hours on the set and then the long hours entertaining clients in the evenings. She was just plain tired and at this particular moment, she was obsessing about the client she had to meet for dinner tonight when she wanted nothing more than to go home and sit on the couch with Corlay and talk of something other than what she felt was a pathetic excuse for a life.

The set was cold and teeming with extras waiting to be part of a crowd scene scheduled for later that day. In the

cavernous sound stage, a small bedroom set sat in the middle of all the chaos. Michelle and Russell Carmichel, who was the current top male B.O.P., were filming a love scene. Russell, who delighted in strutting his well-honed physique, clothed or not, in front of the several hundred extras, grips, and other technical personnel who milled about waiting for director Ripley Jones to set up the next shot, was flexing his biceps while sitting stark naked on the edge of the bed. He'd made a half-hearted attempt to cover himself, but the sheet had slipped.

Michelle closed her eyes and shivered. She drew a thin shirt around herself and squeezed her legs together as she sat primly on the bed's opposite side. There were several more minutes of loud confusion and then someone shouted for places. Jones came to the bed and explained what he wanted. She had to be on top again. The last scene hadn't looked real enough. Russell looked over his shoulder and leered at her and she rolled her eyes.

He lay flat on the bed. "Come on, baby," he crooned. Michelle ignored him and swung her leg across his chest, feeling acutely self-conscious about the feeling of him beneath her. The prop woman arranged the sheets while Jones walked around the bed a few times with the lighting designer, testing angles and light. They walked away and she heard the familiar countdown.

Her face became blank for a moment as she centered herself for the shoot, and then someone yelled, "Action." Russell's hands moved to her thighs and she arched away from him, moving as though he were fully inside her. Her thighs and buttocks ached from the tension of having done this scene fifteen times already and her knees felt like jelly. She let her mind drift, trying to become the character, but there was so little to her that she found it didn't hold her attention. Closing her eyes, she willed herself elsewhere, trying to ignore the reality of what was happening. And suddenly she had a flash of what it might be like to be astride Corlay like this, feeling her move beneath her. In the moment this vision came and went, her body responded, she groaned and Russell got an immediate erection. She felt his penis press against her and cursed.

She cried out in faked orgasmic frenzy and Russell pulled her down to him for the scripted kiss. He smelled of sweat and the garlic he insisted on eating in great quantities and she almost gagged. Then she felt his hands moving on her body as he tried to position her for real — and unscripted — penetration. She pulled back, eyes flashing, and slapped him.

"Cut!" the director screamed, shooting out of his chair like a cannonball. "What the fuck are you doing, Michelle?"

But she hadn't heard him. She was focused fury and her hand was holding Russell's penis in a way that made his eyes bulge out with something that was definitely not pleasure. "—cut it off, I swear," she finished saying in a stage whisper as the director approached. She let go, and Russell scrambled out from underneath her.

Michelle tore the sheet from the bed and wrapped it around her. Then she started shouting. "I've had it," she yelled. "I've fucking had it! Now you listen to me and listen good, Jonesey. First, get my wardrobe mistress down here right now with a robe. Second, close the fucking set to all these goddamn extras. I'm not doing this to give every wanna-be actor a fucking thrill. And third, tell Mr. Carmichel if he ever touches me again in any way that is not called for in the script, I'll cut his fucking dick off and shove it down his

throat!"

She dragged in a sharp breath to keep the tears that threatened at bay. The sound studio was totally silent. "I didn't mean—" Russell began.

"—Shut up," Jones said. Then to Michelle, "Calm down now, okay." He put his arm around her shoulders, but she shrugged it off.

"I'm serious, Ripley. I really am. Don't fuck with me or I'll walk. Contract be damned."

Ripley swallowed. He could not afford to lose her and everyone knew it. They were in the last month of a twelve-month shoot and about two million Credits over budget. More delays would mean getting his butt kicked by the big boys upstairs and he was definitely not in the mood for that. He turned to one of the assistants. "Get Ms. David's wardrobe mistress down here with some clothes right away." Then, in a louder voice he shouted, "Clear the fucking set! Now!"

It took them an hour to clear the extra personnel and placate Russell who was making threats of his own. In the end, they used footage they'd already shot and allowed Michelle to finish the scene in a flesh-colored body suit which would be airbrushed out later. Russell was required to put on a g-string. The entire episode put them nearly four hours behind and when Michelle left for her evening's appointment, some of the crew members, who had been counting on an early night, glared or turned away.

She pretended to ignore them, playing the temperamental star, and strode out to the waiting black limo as the last of the light was lost to evening.

THE WHITE BONES OF TRUTH

❊ ❊ ❊.

Alejandro came into the bedroom he shared with JayJay and sat on the edge of the bed. In the darkness, he could only see the silhouette of JayJay's round form turned away from him toward the wall. He touched her shoulder.

"Go away."

"Please, JayJay. I want to talk to you."

"I'm not interested."

He ignored her and continued speaking. "JayJay, it's not that we don't agree with what you want. You know I'm as sick of this as you. But if we're going to make a difference in the future, we have to be careful now. WKMA is playing *Night Tube* in top rotation. We really have a chance, JayJay, but we can't rush it."

"Kiss My Ass radio. Big fucking deal." She rolled over and looked at him in the evening gloom. "It's getting worse every day, and we're not doing enough to stop it."

"Change takes time," he said in a voice intended to soothe her, but it had the opposite effect.

"Fuck that. Fuck it. No one is really listening to our lyrics, Alejandro. Social change is not going to occur just because WKMA is playing *Night Tube*. It's going to come through direct political action. I'm sick of taking this long route around. I want to go in for the kill. And I want to do it now."

"And throw away everything we've worked for? All our contacts? All the time we've invested in this band? JayJay, this isn't just about me and you anymore. This isn't ten years ago when our names on The List didn't matter so much. This is about something much bigger and there are other people whose safety we're responsible for. We agreed as a

group to do it this way. You agreed. You gave your word. You said you wanted to try and get a Contract and then make changes from the inside."

"Yeah, well, I changed my mind."

"You can't." His voice was hard and serious. "We've come too far to turn back now."

"Fuck you!" she shouted and pushed at him. She raised her fist to hit him, but he made no move to defend himself and she dropped the fist into her lap. "Fuck you," she said more quietly now. "I'm sick of this. All the pretending and the lies. I'm just sick of it."

He reached out to her and this time she came into his arms. "I know," he said quietly. "I know."

"I've been reading the NetBoards. There are a lot of people out there who are really angry."

"I thought you were going to stop surfing for a while."

"Yeah, well ..."

"It's dangerous. You might get caught," Alejandro said.

"I've got my tricks. Come on, I've been on-line for years, Alejandro, and no one's found me yet."

"Security wasn't as strict then."

"You know, you're really pissing me off today," she said, pulling away from him and getting up. "You're being a total wimp. What the hell has gotten into you?"

Alejandro looked away. "I guess I've just been thinking about the fact that if we play our cards right, we could be living the good life."

"That's a bunch of crap and you know it."

"We don't know anything, JayJay. We've heard rumor, that's all. We've never actually seen a Contract."

THE WHITE BONES OF TRUTH

"But it's common knowledge what The Studio is doing. They're just pimping for their stars and making money hand over fist."

"Well, maybe it's not as bad as it sounds."

"Well, maybe it is," JayJay shot back. "Look no one made you promise to stick by my radical side. If you and the others want to sell out, fine. Go ahead. But you can do it without me."

"JayJay, before you get yourself all wound up, would you at least listen to what I'm saying?"

JayJay folded her arms across her breasts and stared at him. Alejandro cleared his throat self-consciously; then he said, "Tell me you've never thought about it, JayJay. Tell me honestly you've never thought about what our lives could be like."

JayJay dropped her hands to her sides and sighed. She went back over to the bed and sat beside her lover. "Of course I've thought about it. I think about it every day. You think I like living like this? In this old warehouse? You think I like eating the crap we have to eat because we can't afford anything else? I would love to be living in some other part of town where the streets are clean and well lit. I'd love to get fresh vegetables and eat meat more than once a month. But unlike the others, and maybe unlike you, I'm not willing to sell out in order to do it." She touched his cheek tenderly. "I love you and I won't stop you if this is what you want. But I can't go with you if you sign, Alejandro. I won't."

"You'd leave me?"

"Don't ask me to choose between you or me, baby, unless you're really ready to hear the answer."

Alejandro shook his head. "So as long as I go along with you—"

"—No. Don't see something that isn't here. My bottom line is this: if you choose to sign a Contract, I won't sign with you. I'm not saying I'll leave you, but I'm not sure I could stay if that were the case. Alejandro, you're a man. You still have most of your personal freedoms intact. I don't. So you can be damned sure I'm going to hold onto the ones I have.

"I love you more than anyone else in the world, but don't ask me to compromise my principles for the sake of money because I won't do it. I can't." There was a long silence. Then Alejandro nodded.

"Okay," he said. "I understand." He reached out for her and she went to him and they lay together, each wrapped in private thoughts, as night dropped down around them.

Alejandro fell asleep some time later, still in his clothes. JayJay, feeling restless, slipped from her place beside him and went into the living room to the Net terminal.

Just as televisions had been an accepted part of the home in the last century, Net terminals were just as popular. JayJay, a veteran hacker, had a system which looked modest to the untrained eye, but over the years, through careful saving, she had managed to create a powerful tool for her second passion in life: NetSurfing.

The basic Net terminal was simply a dumb receiving end much like the old televisions had been. This terminal, which was standard in most houses and apartment complexes, was able to receive signals from over three thousand transmitting television and radio stations and record various audio or visual programs onto an internal hard drive. It also provided Net access. Storage capacity varied according to unit, and JayJay's was relatively small. She didn't need that type of storage as much as she needed to be able to

THE WHITE BONES OF TRUTH

scramble and download information she lifted from the Net.

She slipped on her VR glove and headpiece, flipping the eyepiece down so she could experience the virtual world through as many senses as possible. Powering up, she logged onto the Net under one of her many aliases and started looking around.

JayJay loved playing in this virtual world. Here she could be whatever she wanted — could assume any form or take no form at all. She liked her "invisible" icon best, one that was a shimmer, a suggestion of something there like the shadow of movement caught from the corner of the eye. She loved to watch the reactions of other icons as they brushed too close to her and set off their own proximity alarms while she glided silently by them, laughing.

In the wide corridor that was the main pathway to the NetBoards and other major gathering places, JayJay moved smoothly forward, watching advertisements for hardware, software and even a few new RPGs flash like lightening in her peripheral vision. She turned right at Buddy's Cafe, a gathering place for gamers run by a white dog with a tail shaped like a scimitar. JayJay didn't know the icon's owner, only that the dog, Buddy, always approached new customers with his head tilted to one side and a stupid-ass grin on his narrow canine face. She'd only been in there once, but it was enough. She hated gamers. There was something about them that just didn't seem connected to reality somehow. Always so interested in playing roles in other people's lives, living out some fantasy. She preferred the real world with all its problems and joys.

The corridor narrowed and she slowed in front of a small bulletin board. She lifted an icon-tool from her hip-pack and blew a billowing cloud of fog around her then unscrewed

the right-hand side of the board which revealed another board underneath. Scanning the listings quickly, she found the one she wanted and reached up to unpin it. Just as she was stuffing the paper into her pack, she heard a voice boom, "Where the fuck did all this fog come from?" and moments later, it began to disperse.

JayJay replaced the screw and pulled her cloak of invisibility more tightly around her. As the fog cleared, she saw two icons approach the board. Two men. Dressed in brown leathers, they were supposed to represent mercenaries. It was part of a very popular game right now, a variation on the old hero-quest scenario. One lifted a huge paw of a hand toward the board and pointed, then laughed. The other joined him. They removed several notices and turning swiftly, faded back into the corridor.

Just as JayJay was about to move, she noticed another figure approaching. A man or woman, it was hard to tell, for the cut of the clothes revealed nothing. Dark boots and black pants, a black cape lined in vermillion. As the figure approached, JayJay caught the flash of a white silk shirt beneath the cape. The figure carried something under one arm and as it drew nearer, JayJay saw it was an ancient Celtic harp.

The newcomer paused at the bulletin board, then lifted the harp. It hung suspended in midair and the most beautiful music JayJay had ever heard filled her ears. She was so enthralled with the tune, in fact, that she failed to notice the other's actions — the parchment the newcomer pinned to the hidden bulletin board, the notices removed. It wasn't until the music ended and the stranger turned to go that JayJay realized that like her fog, the stranger had used a cloaking program to hide her actions. She'd never seen anything so

ingenious and discarding caution, she let herself become visible enough to shimmer in the corridor's virtual light.

"I already knew you were there," the stranger said.

"What are you called?" JayJay asked.

"I am Deth, the High One's harpist."

"Who?"

The one called Deth laughed. "You should read more twentieth century fantasy," it said. "And do you have a name? You look like the tail end of a rainstorm."

JayJay didn't know whether to be offended or delighted. The stranger was the most interesting character she'd met NetSurfing in a long time. "This is my cloak of invisibility," she said.

Deth laughed again. "Not a very good cloak if it allows me to see you."

"You're the first one," JayJay countered. "No one else has been able to see me before."

"Don't count on it." Deth's voice was suddenly serious. "Now is the time to be especially careful, little rainstorm. There are many eyes not so friendly as mine. I have seen you here before and in other forms as well. Once, as I recall, you wore a Medusa head."

"I was a banshee."

"You're confusing your mythology," Deth laughed.

"It was deliberate," JayJay protested, feeling as though she were scrambling to keep up with the stranger. She decided a frontal attack might be best. "Your music is an obvious cloak as well. You've read the other board."

Deth did not respond. A long-fingered hand caressed the harp's exquisite body. "You presume much," Deth said at last.

"Am I correct?"

There was a slight nod, the barest tilt of the head. "I know who you are, my little thunderstorm, in this world and the other. I can tell you this — we work toward the same purpose. But you leave trails. You need to be more careful or you will be caught."

Alejandro's warning came to JayJay again and she shivered. "Will you help us?"

"I am already helping you and all the others. Be patient if you can. But you must be careful. Go now. The watchdogs have already been released. They will be here soon." And with that, the harpist vanished, leaving JayJay standing alone.

She hurried back then, taking the quickest exit home. Back at the warehouse, she turned the encounter over and over in her mind. Finally, she accessed the literature database at UCLA. Deth, she discovered, was a character in a brilliant work of fantasy by a twentieth-century writer, who gave the one who might have been his enemy the thing he most desired. JayJay shut down the database and went to bed. But that night she dreamed of the harpist and was haunted by Deth's music.

The next morning Alejandro found her at the terminal again, but this time she wasn't in the virtual world. She was downloading information from her hip-pack — which in the real world was a black box attached to her system — into a portable compiler. She turned when he came into the room and took the cup of instant coffee he offered her. "Have you been here all night?" he asked.

She shook her head. "A lot of it, though. Remember

THE WHITE BONES OF TRUTH

how I told you I thought I'd found a way to access The Studio's e-mail?" He nodded. "Well, I found out there was a small protest at Screen City about a week ago. Everyone was arrested. Seven actors were publicly reprimanded."

"They'll never work in the industry again."

"Hell, they'll be lucky if they're allowed to pick up trash."

An intricately coded newsletter began to scroll across the screen.

"How can you read this shit?" he asked.

"I can't. But the compiler can. I copied these files from another system. Our compiler will translate it into a language we can understand. You have to know the access code to get into the files."

"How'd you find it out?"

"I made some discrete inquiries. Someone was willing to trade me another password for this one, so we swapped." Alejandro shook his head. JayJay's passion for NetSurfing made him nervous. Prison terms for illegal Net activity started at twenty years without parole. "Alejandro, there're a whole lot of people out there and a lot of them know about the band. Our lyrics are making sense to people who know about Contracts, to people who are hungry for revolution. I got into some Organization files, some really old ones. Remember the coup that failed in the early '20s? The password was State of Independence. Isn't that weird?"

Alejandro just nodded.

JayJay cleared the screen. A line of type scrolled across the Net terminal indicating a message waiting to be read. "I wonder how long that's been there," she mused as the message appeared in full text on the screen. She read it silently first and then said, "Hey, listen to this. *JayJay: I slip*

away/They pay my way/I can nothing say... My life flickers..."

"Shit, JayJay. Somebody knows!"

"Calm down. Knows what? That the band has a hit song right now? Anyone can send me e-mail, Alejandro. If it were the 'keepers, they wouldn't bother being so cryptic. It's a bastardized version of *Night Tube*. Look at the first three lines. It's some weird version of the chorus without the repeated line. Look, there's more. *Michaelangelo's "David" was sculpted to look natural to an observer standing below the work. Then, as now, there is always a distortion of reality. Would like to exchange. But not on-line. Interested? Hang a black bandanna in the north window.*"

"Weird," Alejandro said. "*My life flickers.* Someone from The Studio?"

"Yeah," JayJay said. "Maybe. Think we should?"

"No. But you'll do it anyway."

JayJay grinned at him. "You know me too well."

Corlay pushed back from the computer terminal in Michelle's apartment and looked at her watch. It was nearly midnight. She rubbed the back of her neck, thinking of Michelle and wondering when she would be home. She pulled the VR glove slowly from her hand and flexed cramped fingers. Then she eased the headpiece from her brow and stored both in the padded carrybag at her feet. She'd been on the Net for nearly six hours, but only the last few minutes had been at all worthwhile.

She smiled slowly. She had suspected Jennifer Jonston was the shimmer she'd felt on the Net for some time but hadn't been able to trace. She hoped her warnings tonight would be enough to scare Jennifer into being more cautious. They were so close now. So close to the beginning of a new era and she was afraid this drummer, with all her fiery passion, would lose her patience with the slow wheels of change just as things were really coming together.

Confirming the woman's identity had been her first task and, that complete, she could not proceed to the second step — finding a way to bring the musician into her confidence and learn what she knew. Someone had been lifting e-mail messages from The Studio's vault and Corlay was pretty sure it was this little rainstorm. But the reasons behind it eluded her.

Jennifer Jonston did not strike Corlay as unintelligent. And even though Corlay had made it sound as though her disguise wasn't working, it had, actually, taken Corlay some months and a lot of persistence to penetrate it. Most people, outside the NetWatchdogs, wouldn't bother. But Corlay wanted — no needed — to know.

She thought of her own disguise, carefully chosen and meticulously detailed. Deth was all the things Corlay believed she was not. The perfect foil for Corlay. Sighing, she rose and stretched. She looked at her watch again, a feeling of dread growing in the pit of her stomach.

She tried to calm her nerves by recalling that Michelle had said shooting often ran late. But there was something else bothering her tonight. Just a feeling, but one she couldn't seem to shake.

Finally, knowing sleep would elude her, she curled up with one of Michelle's bound books and waited for her to come home.

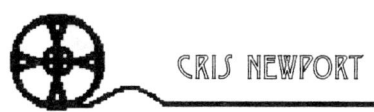 CRIS NEWPORT

✻ ✻ ✻

The woman across the table from Michelle gazed at Michelle over the top of her wine glass with a smirk which meant only one thing. She raised a slender, well-manicured hand and signalled for the check.

In her Power Car, the woman, whose name Michelle thought was Caroline, reached over and planted her hand on Michelle's knee. Michelle looked out the window and sighed. She felt cheap. The memories of Corlay's touch, of Corlay's stories and her gentle comforting presence filled her. She tried to imagine it was Corlay's hand resting so heavily on her leg, but could not. Trying to block out her feelings, she stared at the road ahead. She wanted to shut down. Wanted to feel nothing. She willed her concentration to take her elsewhere. She would not think of Corlay.

Her mind settled and she felt a familiar numbness move slowly from the tips of her fingers until it had settled like a dead icy weight around her heart. She focused on solving algebra problems. That had helped her through many of these evenings before.

They went into the client's apartment. It was tasteful and sparsely furnished. Caroline turned and smiled, beckoning Michelle to follow her into a bedroom. What Michelle saw there when she crossed the threshold made her blood run cold. She took a deep breath to steady her voice and said, "The Contract specifically states bondage is not allowed. Marks show."

Caroline just smiled. She stepped beside Michelle suddenly and pinned her arm behind her. Michelle lost her balance on her spike-heeled shoes and tumbled forward. Caroline dragged her to the bed. Michelle struggled, but she

THE WHITE BONES OF TRUTH

was in an awkward position and this woman was much stronger than Michelle had imagined. "Yes," Caroline whispered harshly, her mouth against Michelle's ear. "Struggle. I love that."

"Please," Michelle said.

"Yes, baby. Please what?" Caroline rolled Michelle over. "Give me your hands," she said. Michelle hesitated, but when she saw Caroline reach for a six-inch hunting knife, she raised her hands in defeat. Caroline snapped Michelle's wrists into handcuffs and then dragged Michelle to her feet again. Shoving her forward, Caroline positioned Michelle in front of a plain wooden door, pulled her arms over her head and attached the three-inch chain between the cuffs to a metal hook imbedded in the door. The muscles in Michelle's arms started to burn and she found it difficult to stay on her feet.

"Kick your shoes off," Caroline commanded and turned her back. Michelle hesitated, knowing that without the extra height her heels provided she would be unable to lift the cuffs off the hook, but then complied, feeling cooperation was probably better in the long run, her mind racing as she tried to come up with a way out. She had never been in a situation like this before. Clients were carefully screened. How could this be happening?

Caroline turned to face her again, hunting knife held loosely in her right hand. She came toward Michelle and Michelle closed her eyes. It was over, she told herself. She didn't think she'd live to see the dawn.

But the woman only slit Michelle's dress up the front and peeled the two sides open as though she were unwrapping a package. Michelle felt relief flood her when the woman dropped the knife onto the carpeted floor. She was naked before Caroline. "I don't want to do this," Michelle

said firmly, trying to distract her.

"Too bad. I paid seven thousand Credits for this."

"You don't understand. You can't do this. The Contract—"

"—Fuck the Contract." Caroline's eyes were hard and filled with rage. "Who the fuck do you think you are? You're just a fucking flicker, Michelle David. But you're just like the rest of us, aren't you? You're not better than any of us. Hey, I've seen your films. You like the rough stuff. I saw your face in *Twelve Ways to Die*. You love this shit."

"That was a movie. It's not real."

Caroline's eyebrows shot up in surprise. "Maybe not, flicker. But this is." Caroline's face came close to hers then. Her breath smelled metallic. Michelle struggled again as Caroline's mouth came down over hers. Her tongue probed against Michelle's teeth. Then a hand clamped her jaw, forced it to open. She felt something cold against her leg. Caroline's hand pushed her thighs apart and the woman's fingers probed her.

Michelle tried to cry out, but no sound came. She thrashed, but this only seemed to excite Caroline more. "Stop," Michelle whimpered. "Please stop." But Caroline did not stop.

After a time, Michelle stopped fighting. Her jaw ached from where Caroline's fingers had bruised it. Caroline was breathing harshly now and the burning in Michelle's groin was familiar. It was like the old days, the early days before Saundra had told her about lubricants. She hadn't had time to use them tonight, hadn't had time for anything. She'd been caught off guard, vulnerable. Part of her blamed Corlay. Corlay had touched something in her she'd buried. It had made her careless. But it wasn't Corlay's fault. In fact, she

THE WHITE BONES OF TRUTH

imagined sinking into Corlay's arms when this horror ended and crying until she was empty. Corlay would comfort her. She had to.

Tears leaked out from beneath closed lids. She withdrew to a small dark place inside herself and waited for it to be over. It had to be over sometime, didn't it?

Suddenly the weight was gone from her chest and the woman was moving away. She was gone for a long time, and when she came back, she uncuffed Michelle without a word. Michelle rubbed her chaffed wrists and tried to arrange the ruined dress around her. It was no use.

In the outer room, she retrieved her trench coat and pulled it firmly around herself. She was shaking and everything hurt. Caroline followed her and for one horrifying minute, Michelle thought she would be captured again. She stumbled, reaching blindly for the door. But the woman only opened it and said, "You're a lousy fuck." She pushed Michelle into the hallway and slammed the door behind her. For a long moment Michelle leaned against the wall, her breath coming in ragged gasps. Then she pushed herself upright and left the building.

Outside, she realized she didn't know where she was. PowerCars slid by on the unkempt street. A breeze picked up, throwing newspapers and trash against the sides of dirty brick buildings. She began to walk north, hoping she'd see a Tube station.

From out of the shadows between buildings, a ragged man slipped into the street behind her. Michelle could see the bright lights of a Tube station about five blocks away. She could also hear the uneven steps of her pursuer. Without slowing, she fumbled in her bag for her StunGun.

The sound of her heels on the pavement echoed in the

empty street. The clumping steps of the man following her grew closer. She could almost feel him behind her and whirled when he grabbed her arm. He struck with his open fist and the StunGun flew out of her hand. They went down on the street together.

His fetid breath pushed into her face. He was covered with oozing sores, and his fingernails, hard and long, scrabbled at her clothing. She screamed.

Kicking herself out from under him, she scanned the dim street. The man lay in a ragged heap, hands clutching the place she'd kicked him. She saw the StunGun, lying in the gutter and made a dash for it. But he uncoiled like a snake and reached it first. He held it in his hands as though he didn't know what it was. Then he turned the barrel towards her. "No!" she cried.

He fired.

She felt the piercing shock of the gun's electric current shoot through her body. She crumpled to the ground. Unable to move and barely conscious, she felt him lean over her. Keeping her eyes closed, she tried to focus her strength on one well-placed kick. He leaned toward her. She tried to bring her leg up, but the StunGun had paralyzed her. She saw his hands coming closer and tried to roll away. Then suddenly, he howled with pain and fell out of her field of vision.

After that, she lost consciousness.

❊ ❊ ❊

Street Captain Madeline Mahoney clicked her helmet into place. Through the smoked face plate, everything looked as though it was enshrouded in a permanent fog. She checked

THE WHITE BONES OF TRUTH

the helmet's rearview detectors, ran a test of the implanted microphone.

The Peacekeeper uniform fit snugly against her short muscular body. She flexed her biceps at herself in the mirror and smiled. It was a perfect world, she thought, as she pushed out of the bathroom at Central Headquarters.

On the street, the silence inside the helmet seemed to shield her from the outside. She walked down the deserted street whistling softly to herself, enjoying the feeling of her toned and powerful muscles pushing her along. She was ready for some action tonight, pumped up for something to happen. So when she heard the unmistakable electric sizzle of a StunGun firing, she ran towards it with glee.

When she got to the scene, however, she was disappointed. No street brawl to deal with. Just a lone sickie and some female who was obviously in the wrong part of town.

The woman had been hit full in the chest and was still jerking a little. Her coat had fallen open and Madeline saw her dress had been slit up the front. "Fucking weirdo," she said. The sickie was reaching for her. "Back off!" she shouted into the microphone. Her voice boomed into the deserted street and bounced off walls. The sickie hesitated and straightened, looking for the origin of the sound. His mouth worked, but no sound came from it. He pointed the StunGun in her direction. Perfect, she thought, grinning, and raised her own weapon.

She fired and he was thrown five feet back and landed with an audible grunt. He twitched and shuddered as if with seizure. She loved this part, watching these bastards soil themselves while staring helplessly up into her face. A light rain started to fall and she switched on the defogger

mechanism in her helmet, then waited, hands on hips, for him to finish seizing.

He did and his mouth worked. She saw ruined teeth. "Got it from a needle, didn't you?" she asked him. Without giving him time to answer, she said, "You know once you become Terminal, you're not allowed on the streets. What were you thinking, friend?" Her voice took on a soothing edge, but she could tell by the expression on his face he thought of her as anything but. "Now, where are you supposed to be?"

He groaned at her, making an attempt to reach into one of his pockets, but she kicked at his hand. "No funny stuff, asshole," she snapped. "I don't have time for this shit. You know the laws. And it's your own damn fault you got it in the first place. Probably refused treatment, didn't you? Just wanted your next fix? Well, asshole, you had your chance. And now, you're luck's all gone."

His ruined face stared up at her. She made sure he was making eye contact before she raised the .45 that had been her mother's and shot him in the face. When his head exploded, splattering gore across the rain-slick street, she smiled. One less Rush addict in the world was just fine with her.

She left his body in the street and stepped away. Taking out her CleansingKit she wiped her suit off slowly. She knew she'd have to go through Decontam when she got back to Headquarters to get the rest of the gore off, but this would do for now. Tossing the kit onto the sickie's body, she dropped a flare on top of the whole mess and ignited it. Then she called for backup.

A few minutes later, two squads arrived, followed by a Contamination Unit team. She'd done everything by the

THE WHITE BONES OF TRUTH

book, even though they hated it when the 'keepers set the fires. Fucking pyros, she thought, watching them stare at the black oily smoke rising from the body. She was glad she couldn't smell it. While they dealt with the remains, the backup squad, in full protective gear, lifted the woman into the back of one of the cars. A paramedic checked her over. "Rape," she said and covered her with a blanket.

"By the sickie?" Madeline asked.

"No. Must have happened before."

Madeline shrugged. "Yeah, didn't think he had it in him. Hell, when they're Terminal, they're just walking zombies anyway." But what the fuck was she doing in this neighborhood? Didn't she know a deserted street usually meant you should get off it and inside? The paramedic handed Madeline the woman's purse and Madeline rifled through it unceremoniously. She extracted the ID card. "Fucking flicker," she muttered. "What the hell was she doing out here?"

"Well, whatever it was, she might want to file charges."

"You better take your pictures, then," Madeline said.

The paramedic took a camera from the shelf above her head. She uncovered Michelle and took a series of photos. As they popped out of the camera, she handed them to Madeline, who labelled them for the evidence file.

Michelle David began to wake up. She moaned and her eyes fluttered open. The first thing she saw was the camera's flash and she raised her hands to cover her eyes. The paramedic handed the camera to Madeline. "How do you feel?" she asked.

"Who are you?" Michelle countered.

"Simone Belfizay. I'm a paramedic. Can you tell me

what happened?"

"When?"

"Christ on a crutch," Madeline put in. "Who raped you? The sickie? Or was it someone else?"

"The sickie?"

"The guy on the street."

"No," she said. "No, it wasn't him. It was someone else. A woman."

The paramedic shot Madeline a disgusted look, but Madeline shrugged and said, "We need to take you in."

"No."

"I'm sorry, but it's procedure. And you need to either file charges or sign a waiver." She handed Michelle one of the more graphic photos. "Whoever did this to you needs a serious lesson in politeness. That is, unless it was consensual. If you like this stuff," she finished, trying to sound bored.

"It's complicated," Michelle said.

"I bet it is," Madeline replied. She lifted off her helmet and motioned for the paramedic to wait outside. "You're Michelle David," she said when they were alone. Michelle nodded. "Want to tell me what happened?"

"I need to talk to a lawyer first," Michelle said. "I'm sorry, but that's procedure for us."

Madeline ran a hand through her short hair and Michelle stared at her, trying to read her intent. She seemed a contradiction — all business and distance and yet there was something below that, an anger or frustration that had, Michelle sensed, something to do with her. Or The Studio.

"I'm telling you if you don't let us handle this, it's going to happen again. And you know the law is very explicit about not filing rape charges. You can be fined. Or imprisoned."

THE WHITE BONES OF TRUTH

Michelle nodded. She had a splitting headache and it was difficult to focus. She forced herself to concentrate and speak slowly. "I understand that, but the situation is complicated and I am not at liberty to make this decision myself. Please, I don't want to make your job more difficult, but you need to let me talk to a lawyer and then I'll be able to answer your questions."

Madeline nodded finally. She knew how it would end, had seen it happen before. She rose briskly and jumped out of the back of the vehicle. To the paramedic she said, "Meet me at Headquarters," and then she disappeared into the darkness.

They had given Michelle a synthetic jumpsuit that crackled when she moved. The paramedic had given her something for the pain, but the bruises were already beginning to show on her face and neck. By tomorrow, she would be covered with marks. She severed the connection with The Studio's legal department, left the private conference room, crossed the hall and entered another room where Madeline sat at a scarred table drinking coffee. Her helmet lay on the table nearby and she had changed into a clean uniform.

Michelle sat down and looked at the piece of paper she'd made her notes on. "I wrote it all down for you," she said and then recited the information. "'The Studio will not press charges against the client who allegedly perpetrated this act of sexual violence against one of its Contracted Stars. The Studio accepts the responsibility of the fine which will be imposed at a later date. A bill should be sent to the address below.' It's all there," she said. "They also said after I sign the waver, you're required to release me. I guess there's a bail fund already set up for this precinct and you're supposed to take the money from there. If you have any questions, Justin Mitchell is at this number now." She pushed the paper across the table to Madeline and watched the other woman's nostrils flare in disgust.

"You realize you perpetuate this cycle by doing this," Madeline said at last.

Michelle took a deep breath. She was almost at her wits' end, almost at the end of her endurance. She wanted comfort. She wanted sleep. She did not want to have to justify Studio policies to a beat cop. "I am under Contract. I have to do what they tell me. You must understand that. Don't they have procedures here you have to follow even if you don't agree with them?"

"Of course. But our policies are set up to protect victims, not criminals. Do you have any idea how difficult it was to get this rape legislation passed? How difficult it was to convince the male population that women's bodies and women's lives are valuable? That rape victims shouldn't be the ones who have to defend their histories or have the burden of proof laid upon them? Do you know how many women died from crimes related to battering and rape before this legislation was implemented and how much the current government wants to overturn it? Every time someone opts to pay the fine over pressing charges, or opts to spend a fortnight in prison rather than prosecute, this law loses its power. Pretty soon, it'll be overturned, the same way the abortion law was overturned. Women are becoming property again, Ms. David, and you are making it easier for that to happen."

Michelle felt stricken. She shut her eyes, feeling the walls closing in on her, watching her choices narrow until

there ceased to be any options at all. "I'm sorry," she said finally. "But I must do as I am told."

"Or what? Not be a film star anymore? Not have your condo on the coast? Your limo driver? Your vacations in Europe?"

"Shut up!" Michelle shouted, propelling herself out of the chair. It fell over with a crash. She pounded the table with her fist and yelled, "Until you have even an inkling of what you're talking about, I would advise you to keep your fucking mouth shut! You have no idea what my life is like, 'keeper. You have no idea. And until you do, you have no right to criticize or condemn me. Now give me the goddamn waiver. I want to go home."

Madeline, stunned by the outburst, slid the pad across the table. Michelle signed it angrily and shoved it back. Reaching across the table, she dumped the contents of the evidence bag and began separating items. The photos had to stay with the waiver, she knew from the lawyer's instructions, but her personal items could be claimed. Shoving everything back into the cloth envelope, she velcroed the lip closed and slammed out of the room, leaving Madeline staring at the square color photographs which, in a few days, would be the only evidence of Michelle David's rape.

* * *

CRIS NEWPORT

Chapter 4
Outrageous Sums

CHAPTER FOUR: OUTRAGEOUS SUMS

By the time Phoenix was little more than five hundred feet into the abandoned subway tunnel, the light was all but gone. His feet moved carefully over the uneven ground, sloshing now and then through puddles of standing water. He could hear noises all around him, skittering claws across cement and steel. Rats, he figured, and tried not to dwell on the idea. Years ago, before he'd even been born, these underground tunnels had carried thousands daily to and from their jobs. He tried to imagine the platform he'd tumbled onto crowded with people all waiting for the headlight of the oncoming train, but found it difficult.

He'd seen the old pictures of what Los Angeles had been like once — a city teeming with violence and gang warfare. At one time, more than half of the city's youth population had gang affiliations, the others just tried to keep out of the way. It was a city ruled by the combustion engine, a city dependent on individual transportation. Now what were once called freeways stood as silent reminders of another time. When the strict environmental laws were enacted nearly a quarter century ago, the combustion engine had been outlawed. No one, he remembered from his history lessons, had believed the laws would pass and there was almost a decade of chaotic transition. But soon the PowerCars were everywhere, using forced air jets to keep them afloat, and MagLev transportation for long distances was the norm.

For a while the old freeways became ganglands, and

thousands of hormonally charged adolescents ran rampant up and down the cement highways on contraband motorcycles and motorized skateboards, killing each other with stunning regularity. Then the curfew was enacted. Then the laws allowing Peacekeepers to shoot anyone found on the streets after dark. That, he remembered, curbed gang activity quite effectively.

But that kind of safety had a price. What was once Los Angeles, now called Screen City in homage to the one and only industry which thrived here, was more like a police state than the part of the free country it had once been. In fact, all of what was once California was now part of a consortium of states with its own government and its own Constitution. And although it was still called a democracy, it was in name only. Words change, Corlay had told him once, when he was still quite young and frustrated with his growing understanding of the unfairness in the world.

And so does the culture. What was once accepted was now forbidden, and what was once forbidden was now practiced widely. It seemed much of the contemporary culture was a direct reaction to what it had been before, a pendulum swung to an extreme opposite. He didn't think he'd ever understand that, no matter how much he debated ethics with Corlay or how long he lived.

As he moved cautiously down the dark tunnel, he wondered what it had been like to live in the twilight of the twentieth century, when nearly everyone owned a car and women still had the right to choose what happened to their own bodies. What had it been like before people like Corlay were genetically engineered in a series of experiments aimed, altruistically, at ending the gender wars? But that idea had exploded in the scientists' hands. Now, of the handful of

THE WHITE BONES OF TRUTH

engineered humans, Corlay was one of the only ones still alive. Some of the others had died of complications arising from their bodies' physiological confusion. Some, Corlay had told him, had been murdered because they were so different and therefore so threatening. And then there were those who took their own lives, unable to balance their outcast status with their innately human desires and needs.

He could not imagine what it was like to be Corlay. He could not imagine the strength that lay beneath her quiet and gentle exterior. And he chided himself for his harshness about her films. What else did she have, really? There were few who would be her friend, and Phoenix had learned early on if he wanted to have friends of his own it was better to let them believe he'd been born of two regular humans, the Whitsons, rather than the product of a laboratory experiment which had also created horribly deformed or retarded individuals. Corlay had always called him her miracle. And when he was old enough to understand the implications of the project, he knew he was.

Longing for her made his chest tight. She was his rock, his reason for fighting back against a system he felt was wrong. She was the center of his existence; he could not imagine loving another as he loved the androgyne who had created him solely out of her own flesh and spirit. He would find his way back to her, no matter what.

Up ahead, a dim light bloomed in the darkness. Startled, Phoenix halted his slow progress and stared ahead, trying to make out shapes in the blurred distance. The tunnel was silent save for his own breathing and after a few moments of heart-pounding fear, he realized he'd merely come to another platform, another stop on the underground system.

When he reached the platform and climbed the rusty ladder leading from the tunnel's bed to the platform floor, he began scouting around for a way out. As with the other platform, the main exit had been bricked over. He walked up and down, testing rusted metal gates and prying loose stone blocks from the walls in the hopes he would uncover something useful.

But after an hour's search, he realized he'd have to keep moving. Climbing back down into the tunnel again, he began to walk. Then, glancing to his right, it occurred to him he hadn't explored the other side of the tracks. So he pushed through a narrow opening separating the two lengths of silver metal and climbed onto the opposite platform. There, he found an iron ladder imbedded in the concrete wall which disappeared into a dark round opening above his head. He started up.

The darkness closed in around him and he had to use all his powers of concentration to keep from panicking. Sticky strands of spiderwebs brushed across his hands and face and he expected at any moment to strike his hands or head against the sealed opening he imagined above him.

After what seemed like an eternity, he began to hear sound. A rhythmic thumping that started and stopped. He continued to climb and the sounds became clearer. It was music. Far above his head, a dim shaft of light shone down in the shape of a large square C. He climbed quickly toward it and came at last to a metal trap door above him. He pushed, but it didn't move. The music above him was louder now and sounded vaguely familiar. He pushed again without success. Then he started banging on the door with his fist and shouting.

The music stopped abruptly. He could hear muffled

THE WHITE BONES OF TRUTH

voices. He banged again. "Hey, anybody up there? Can you hear me?"

"Where are you, man?" a voice asked.

He pounded again. "Here. Under the trap door."

"What trap door?" There was the sound of general chaos above him, boots scraping over the floor, something heavy being dragged. Then there was a sudden scream of unoiled metal and he was blinded by daylight streaming down upon him.

He looked up into the barrel of a StunGun. Blinking, he raised one hand, palm visible. "Hey. Hello. I got trapped in the underground by accident and I'm just trying to find my way out. I'm unarmed."

The gun's barrel wavered and someone said, "Let him up, Danny-o." And then strong arms were lifting him out of the dark passage and onto the floor. He coughed and rubbed his tearing eyes which were beginning to adjust to the light. "I'm Alejandro Jardines," the man who had pulled him up said.

"Phoenix Whitson."

"This is Jennifer Jonston, Kay Leemer and Danny O'Brien." When Danny-o was introduced, he lowered the StunGun reluctantly. After a moment, when it became clear Phoenix was not going to kill or attack them, he put the gun away. Alejandro kicked the trap door back into place and bolted it. "I always wondered where that led to," he mused and bent to replace the rug.

"Yeah, well, it's not very interesting down there. I wouldn't recommend it."

Alejandro laughed. "I'll take your word for it. Come on, you must be starved and you certainly could use a bath."

❄ ❄ ❄

Phoenix cradled a cup of coffee in his hands. The smooth white porcelain was a reassuring weight and he walked to the window with it to stare out at the deep blue sky. Although the warehouse's windows were grimy, dense afternoon light streamed in like golden warmth and he stood, watching the steam from the cup rise, thinking of Corlay and worrying.

His eyes rested on three black bandannas taped to the window. They didn't seem to have any purpose and when JayJay came back into the room with a mug of her own, he asked her about them. "We got a message from a flicker ... sorry," she apologized when he grimaced, "from a film Star who wants to exchange information with us. She told us to put a black bandanna in the window if we wanted to talk."

"So you put up three just to be on the safe side?"

JayJay laughed. "Alejandro's idea. Not mine."

"How do you know it's a she?"

"We know who it is, actually. She didn't cover her electronic tracks well enough and I traced it. It's Michelle David."

Phoenix's eyes widened. "No kidding. My ... guardian knows her."

"Well?"

"Well enough," he hedged, realized JayJay's piercing eyes had caught his hesitation. "What kind of information?" he asked, feigning nonchalance.

"Phoenix," JayJay laughed softly. "Did you know you're named for a mythical bird that rose from the ashes of chaos?"

He nodded.

THE WHITE BONES OF TRUTH

"Was it deliberate, then?"

Again, the nod.

"You know something, don't you?" she prodded gently.

"About what?"

"You're a bad liar, Phoenix-Who-Rises-From-The-Ashes. All right. Let me ask you this ... what do you know about us?"

"I know your song is getting a lot of airplay right now. And ..." he paused and hesitated, then plunged on, "that the lyrics seem to hint at something. Something about Contracts."

"Very perceptive of you," she said. "We have heard rumors about what the Contracts demand," she continued slowly, testing his reaction to her words. "And we would like to separate truth from rumor."

"For what purpose?" Phoenix asked.

"I'm not convinced," she said carefully, "that the Contracts are in the best interests of those who sign them."

Phoenix relaxed visibly, then tensed again. "A lot of people say that," he countered. "But few are willing to put their reputations on the line to take a stand in public."

"But you are."

"Yes," he said, his chin lifting as his eyes burned into hers. "I am."

She laughed out loud at him, and Phoenix felt anger rising. He opened his mouth as if to speak, but she waved him to silence, her expression serious. She stepped close to him and said in a conspiratorial whisper, "Phoenix Whitson, we know your name is on The List. We know we harbor a criminal of the State. If we were not willing to put ourselves in harm's way, you would already be in the custody of the

'keepers." She stepped back and spoke normally again. "We are in a unique position right now, Phoenix, as there's a good chance Oilslick Records is going to offer us a Contract in the near future. And if they do, we have the opportunity to make changes from the inside."

"What makes you think it'll work?"

"Revolution doesn't always have to come from the outside."

"That's what my guardian, Corlay, says too. But I'm telling you, JayJay, this time you're wrong."

Now it was JayJay's turn to bristle at another's words. "What makes you so knowledgeable about this? You haven't signed a Contract or you wouldn't dare be here."

"You're right. I haven't. But my closest friend has. And I know. You can't change it once it's signed, JayJay. It'd be better if the whole system was just destroyed and we started again from scratch."

JayJay forced herself to take a deep breath, to not be judgmental or rash at this moment, but instead to take the young man at his word. "What are you willing to tell me?" she asked.

"What are you offering?"

"Safe haven. One meal a day for as long as you care to stay. More if you can contribute something to household expenses."

"I can't access my Credits. I'm sure the account's been frozen at least temporarily and any attempt would lead them right to me. But I will tell you what I know in exchange for a place to sleep and whatever food you can spare."

JayJay extended her hand and they sealed the agreement. Phoenix finished the coffee and settled himself on one of the cushions strewn about the practice space. "This is

THE WHITE BONES OF TRUTH

what I know," he said and told her.

When he was finished, she whistled. "I'd guessed a lot of it, but not everything." She cursed under her breath and pushed herself into a standing position. "I need to talk to Alejandro. Make yourself at home. Dinner's at six in the downstairs kitchen." She left him then, and Phoenix returned to the windows. He pushed one of them open and let the hot, dry air rush over him. He thought of Robert, missed him, wondered if he had been released yet and how much bail The Studio would charge to his account. Shaking his head, he swirled the coffee grounds around the bottom of the cup. All he could do for the moment was sit and wait. And try and figure out what to do next.

Danny-o and Kay arrived for dinner just before six. They lived together, though not as lovers, in an apartment adjacent to the warehouse. At one time, the band had all shared a loft space, but it had become clear early on if the band was going to survive, they would have to live separately even if it meant an increase in rent.

Everyone worked odd jobs, and Credits were pooled to buy groceries and pay other bills. Danny-o's cigarettes and beer came out of whatever money he had left over after expenses. Today, Kay had managed to get in a few hours work at the beauty salon in a neighboring district and she came in with a bag of essential items — bread, canned soup and toilet paper — which she put away without speaking. "I took our cut," she explained to JayJay who only nodded.

Dinner was meager. Everyone got a small bowl of heated soup and a few spoonfuls of boxed macaroni and cheese. Water to drink from the tap. Everyone ate in silence, and Phoenix found himself thinking of Corlay's well-stocked freezer and of the Whitsons' ability to serve him meat

whenever he ate with them. This was not his first exposure to the way people on the other end of the economic spectrum lived, but for the first time he understood that this could well become his life. That he might not ever be able to see Corlay again. He gazed around the kitchen and felt a deepening funk come over him. They sat in five mismatched chairs at a fake wood table pitted with burns and scars. Their bowls and plates were thin recycled plastic, the spoons a kind of pressed aluminum that indicated they'd been made from old carbonated drink cans. Danny-o got up suddenly from the table and extracted a generic beer from a cooler pushed into the corner under a table that served as counter space. He didn't offer one to anyone else and Phoenix didn't ask.

After a few more minutes, Alejandro rose and put a kettle of water on. He pulled out a large plastic jar of instant coffee and gestured. "Who wants?"

Phoenix found his voice, "Me, please." He looked at JayJay. She was scraping the last of the cheese mixture from her plate with a piece of white bread. When she found him looking at her, she smiled.

"Had enough?" she asked.

He nodded. "Thanks. I know it's not easy to feed—"

Alejandro cut him off. "We can do this right now, Phoenix. We are all working part-time jobs and making a little money off our music. It is not the best cuisine, but it takes the hunger away."

"A few years ago I would have killed for a meal like this," Kay said. "But now," she pushed her spoon around an empty bowl, "it doesn't seem like enough."

"It won't be much longer," JayJay put in. "I can feel it."

Danny-o scoffed and got a second beer out of the

THE WHITE BONES OF TRUTH

cooler.

"If you're going to drink yourself stupid again," JayJay said, "go home. You're such an asshole when you're drunk."

"Fuck you," he muttered and popped open the can.

"She means it," Alejandro put in, not turning from where he was filling mugs with steaming water. He turned and set one of the mugs down before Phoenix with a packet of instant milk and sugar. "And so do I. You've really got to decide, Danny-o, what you want more — the band or the beer."

Danny-o looked at Alejandro. "Who died and made you God?"

Alejandro shrugged and turned away. "The deadline's coming up, you know," he said evenly. "Next week."

"I remember the fucking deadline. Jesus, you think I'm a moron or what?"

"You don't really want me to answer that, do you?" JayJay said.

Danny-o pushed back from the table so violently that coffee sloshed out of mugs and his beer can fell over. "Fuck you. Fuck all of you." And then he was gone, slamming the door behind him.

Phoenix just stared after him. Kay laid a hand on his arm and said, "Don't pay any attention to him. He just does it to get attention."

"What, drink?" Phoenix asked, mopping up spilled coffee with a rag Alejandro handed him.

"No. That's a real addiction. The temper tantrums. Happens all the time."

"But what about this deadline?"

"Next week. He has to either stop drinking or quit the

band. We've given him a lot of chances over the years, Phoenix," JayJay explained, "but this is the last one."

"Why don't you just commit him to rehab? That's still a federally funded program."

"Yeah. But we'd probably never see him again. They'd ship him out-of-state to whatever facility had an opening. When you come out, unless you've got the money to get back to where you came from, a job and someone to vouch for you there, they'll find you a job wherever you did rehab and there you stay. Rehab's a one-time shot. He's our friend. We don't want to abandon him."

Phoenix nodded. "I understand," he said.

Just then, there was a pounding at the door. Phoenix looked around, his eyes wide with fright. JayJay said calmly, "Go with Alejandro. This has happened before. He'll show you where to hide. They won't find you. Don't worry. Kay, you'd better look domestic. Why don't you start on the dishes?"

Alejandro and Phoenix went swiftly from the room while JayJay went to the door. She looked through the peephole and saw two men in suits standing in the harsh light of the hallway's naked bulb. "Can I help you?" she said into the speaker next to the door.

"We're from Oilslick Records," one said.

"Yeah, sure, and I'm Jesus Christ," she muttered. "Put your IDs in the drawer." She shoved open a drawer they'd stolen from an abandoned night depository and installed in the wall next to the door. She heard a thump as something fell into the drawer and she pulled it back to examine the IDs.

They looked legit. Alejandro came up beside her then, took the offered IDs and riffled quickly through them. He nodded and she opened the door. The two men stepped into

THE WHITE BONES OF TRUTH

the living area and Alejandro handed them back their IDs. The taller of the two suits stuck out his hand. "Oskar Rabinowitz," he said. He was about twenty-five, clean-shaven with a buzz cut popularized by the middle-of-the-road political factions. It was a haircut that said: I'm cool but not uptight. JayJay took his hand. It was slightly sweaty and she wondered if this was his first time in the warehouse district.

The other man, who also sported a buzzcut, introduced himself as Rafe Zidrikson. He clearly knew the routine. He loosened his tie immediately upon shaking hands with them and grinned as if trying to put them at ease. "Cool place," he said, eyeing the bare walls painted industrial green and the sparse battered furnishings. "How you like livin' down here?" he asked. He had the slightest trace of a Southern accent, one that even the best vocal schools could not erase. That was a real shame, JayJay thought, wondering how many jobs it had cost him. It was a black mark these days to be from the South and try and work anywhere else. After the southern states had finally seceded from the rest of the country at the turn of the century and closed their borders to all non-whites, not many people would even associate with Southerners, much less hire one, no matter what the individual's personal politics. It was good riddance, most said. He was only the second Southerner she'd ever met and the very fact of his background made her immediately suspicious.

"Fine," she replied even though she knew the question had been addressed to Alejandro. She gestured to the living room. "You gentlemen want to come in and make yourselves comfortable? What can we do for you tonight?"

Rafe reached into the pocket of his suit coat and drew out a computer pad. JayJay knew what it was even before he

said it. A Contract. "Well," he said slowly, "we've been authorized by Oilslick Records to offer you a recording Contract."

He handed the computer pad to Alejandr,o who took it without looking at it. Rafe withdrew a stylus next. "You need to sign at the end."

"We need to read it over first," JayJay put in. Alejandro shot her a warning glance and she fell silent.

"You will not begrudge us this?" Alejandro asked softly.

"We'll just wait."

"I'm afraid that won't be possible. You see, our guitarist is not here right now and we can't sign anything without his permission. You understand this, of course?" Rafe nodded. If it had been Kay, it would have been different, but Danny-o's gender had bought them some time. "I will bring this to your office personally tomorrow, yes?"

"I don't know," Oskar began. "The bosses, you know, don't like any unauthorized access." He looked at JayJay. "If you get my drift." JayJay's look shot daggers into his flesh and he paled.

"Well." Alejandro rose. He started to hand the pad back. "Then I am afraid we must decline. Danny-o is an integral part of this band, the lead guitarist. I would not presume to make a decision without consulting him. I'm sure your bosses will understand. You might also want to tell them Screen City Recording Company has made us an offer which is, shall we say, very generous. You might want to tell your bosses that."

Rafe's face was grim. He fumbled in his suit coat for a moment before extracting a palm-sized cellular phone. "You won't mind if I just call and confer with the head of

THE WHITE BONES OF TRUTH

Contracts, will you?"

Alejandro grinned and shook his head. "Not at all."

Rafe walked to the far end of the room and turned his back. He spoke softly and rapidly into the phone. JayJay studied Oskar, mentally undressing him in an obvious way and enjoying his discomfort. She hated suits. Alejandro shot her another warning look and she shrugged at him. Kay came in from the kitchen drying her hands as Rafe walked back toward them.

"We need it by tomorrow, noon."

"That will be acceptable," Alejandro said. "I would like my lawyer to look it over as well."

Rafe grunted and gestured to Oskar. Clearly this was not the way he had anticipated the meeting would go. Alejandro got up with the Contract in his hand and walked toward the door. The two men followed. They shook hands again and Alejandro closed the door behind them.

Kay was the first to pounce on him. "You almost cost us the fucking Contract. What were you thinking?" she shrieked.

"I cost us nothing," he said. "You want to settle for whatever bones they throw us? That's your business. But I don't. You don't know what this says, Kay."

"But you acted as if —"

"You have to be willing to give up everything," Alejandro said dryly and then grinned. He shook the pad over his head. "We did it!" he shouted. "We did it."

Kay launched herself at him and he caught her in a bear hug. JayJay, fuming on the couch, said nothing. Then she stomped out of the room, coming back with Phoenix a moment later. Alejandro was in the kitchen working the cork out of a half bottle of champagne they'd been saving for this

occasion. It popped out and hit the wall just above Phoenix's head. "What the hell?" he asked, watching Alejandro pour champagne into four small glasses.

"We got a Contract offer," Kay yelled. "A real Contract."

JayJay and Phoenix exchanged glances. Alejandro thrust the glasses into their hands. "A toast," he cried. "To the future." He raised his glass and drank. The others did the same. JayJay said nothing while Phoenix offered his congratulations. Alejandro drained his glass and said to Kay, "Go find Danny-o. He's probably down at The White Boar. Get his ass up here so we can go over this thing." Kay scampered from the room.

Alejandro sat down at the table and looked up at JayJay. "You don't seem very excited," he said.

"You seem to have forgotten our earlier conversation."

"Let's just see what it says before we go jumping to conclusions, okay?"

JayJay nodded. She pulled up a chair. "Let's see this damn thing," she said.

Two hours later the light had all but faded from the sky. The lamp on the table was on and JayJay and Alejandro were stretching cramped muscles. Phoenix, pouring hot water into cups for their third round of coffee, said, "I don't like it. It sounds like the same shit Robert's embroiled in."

"I don't know, Phoenix. It seems pretty straight forward to me. They give an advance and then you pay it back."

"But it's not that simple," Phoenix argued, bringing the mugs to the table. "Once you get into debt, they make sure you never get out. Remember those credit card scams of the twentieth century? The problem of revolving credit? People got themselves into thousands of dollars worth of debt and then ended up only being able to pay on the interest and not the principle. It's the same thing here, Alejandro. Don't be fooled by the advance. What if the disc doesn't sell? What if it's poorly marketed? You have no say over how it's marketed, the cover art, anything. You don't even have say over the arrangements." He keyed to the end of the document and read, "*The Company reserves the right to make final decisions on all arrangements, which includes but is not limited to instrumentation and lyrics.* They can tell you what to sing, Alejandro. Is that what you want?" Alejandro didn't reply. "You can't change this system from the inside. You just can't."

"What if we amend the Contract?" JayJay asked.

"Amend it how?" Alejandro put in.

"Write in what we want. Change the parts we don't like. Cross out the bullshit about final decisions and send it back to them unsigned. Tell them we'll sign if they make those changes."

"That's a big risk," Alejandro said.

"No bigger than your lie about Screen City Recording," she countered. "Look, I'm not going to sign this as is—"

"—what do you mean?" It was Danny-o's voice. He was leaning against the door frame to the kitchen and now he came into the room with the pronounced swagger which belied his drunkenness. "Of course you're going to sign it. Or if you don't, we'll sign it in your stead. Don't forget who the band leader is here, girl."

"Danny-o," Alejandro cautioned.

"No, man. Fuck it. I've taken just about enough of

this feminist bullshit. You forget, JayJay, you don't have veto rights in this band. The agreements have always been in my name and Alejandro's. You have to do what we say."

"You forget, asshole, that without me you don't have a band," JayJay shot back.

"Oh, but JayJay, that's not true," he crooned, his voice oily. "You have to stay in this band. It's the law and you know it."

"Fuck you!" she screamed. "You forget you can barely carry a tune and we've been carrying you for too damn long. You're replaceable, Daniel O'Brien, and you know it. And it makes you sick, doesn't it?" She was right in his face now, her breath hot on his cheek. "You just can't decide what you love more —the band or the bottle. But the bottle always wins. You run away when it gets hard while the rest of us slog through.

"You're an irresponsible prick and you know it. That's what really eats away at you, doesn't it? It's not this 'feminist bullshit', it's the fact that you can't get sober. That in the long run it'll be the comforting stupor you choose instead of your friends."

"We care about you, Danny-o," JayJay said, her voice suddenly less angry. "But I know I'm tired of not being able to rely on you, of you not pulling your weight around here, with the band or the household responsibilities. You're not a kid anymore. It's time to grow up."

Danny-o just stared at her for a long moment as if stunned both by the fury and the meaning of her words. For one moment he seemed vulnerable and scared, and then a wall crashed down behind his eyes again and his face grew hard with anger. "You little bitch," he snarled. "You think just because you've convinced Alejandro that you're God, the

rest of us will fall in line. Well, I've got news for you. I don't buy it."

JayJay shook her head, her mouth a tight line of frustration. She watched Danny-o wobble as he pulled back to strike her. The sad part, she thought, is that this isn't even a fair contest. Her fist shot out, connecting with his jaw with a resounding crack. Danny-o tumbled backward like a pile of sticks and landed on the floor with a thump. JayJay swore and rubbed her hand. "Shit, that hurt!"

Kay rushed over to him. "Did you have to do that? You know he doesn't know what he's saying when he's drunk."

"I'm sick of that excuse, Kay. Quit sticking up for him. He's not worth it."

Kay crumpled on the floor next to him. "I want the Contract, JayJay. I want it. I'm tired of being hungry all the time. I'm tired of getting my clothes from the second-hand store, wearing other people's cast-offs. I want something in this life, JayJay, and this is my one big chance. And you're going to fuck it up for all of us. You're so goddamn selfish. You—" her words were cut off by sobs.

JayJay started to go to her, but Alejandro stepped between them. He pulled her aside and whispered, "Let me talk to them, okay? Can you try and keep your temper under control for just twenty-four hours until we figure out what to do?" JayJay nodded, feeling admonished. "Look, I agree we can't sign this as is and our best bet is probably to just send it back with the changes, but let me talk with Sam tomorrow, okay? Let me see what he says about our legal rights and what kind of bargaining power we do or don't have. Can you just let me do that, JayJay?"

"Yes," she said quietly. She rubbed absently at her

throbbing fist. "I'm sorry. It's just that he pisses me off."

"I know. But shit, JayJay." Alejandro gestured to where Danny-o lay sprawled and shook his head. "I'm going to take them home and get Danny-o to bed. Don't wait up for me. I'll stop by in the morning before I go see Sam, all right?"

JayJay nodded. She put her arms around him. "I love you," she said into his chest.

"I love you, too. Even though you have a terrible temper."

She laughed and hugged him tighter, then released him. He bent down and picked up Danny-o from where he was splayed like a boneless scarecrow and slung him over his back. "Come on, Kay," he said as if speaking to a child. "Let's get you home." She rose from the floor in silence and followed him out the door.

JayJay sank into a chair at the kitchen table. "Shit," she said without conviction. "What a fucking mess." Phoenix, who had been silent throughout this whole ordeal, pulled up a chair and joined her. She looked up at him and said, "Do you really think Oilslick would amend their Contract to meet our demands?"

"Honestly? I doubt it. There are just too many hungry people out there. They can find someone who will swallow the whole thing without question. Why work with a group that promises to be difficult?"

"Money?"

"Maybe. But that's a real risk. The public is fickle. What's hot one day is passe the next. Right now you're pushing the envelope with your lyrics. You're taking risks that make people feel like they're part of something illicit, something slightly illegal. And that's a rush. But when push comes to shove, they're not going to let you really talk about

THE WHITE BONES OF TRUTH

what's going on. They're not going to let you sing about the corruption of a system you would now be part of. I don't think you can get what you want out of this deal, JayJay."

"So you're saying we should either sign the Contract and live well, if in incredible debt, for the rest of our lives or fold."

"Those are your options. Remember, debt is passed down if you can't pay it off. It goes to your heirs, your estate. Your kids are going to have to pay for your lifestyle or somewhere down the road Oilsilck's going to let you take a fall that'll cost you everything. Maybe even your life."

"What are you saying?"

"There have been so-called accidents involving popular Stars and performers. The Studio has to recoup their losses somehow, especially if someone is getting out of control. Or they'll just freeze your accounts until you cooperate. You don't work. You don't eat. And you can't work for anyone else, either. You're blacklisted, JayJay." He pushed back a little in his chair. "It doesn't seem like a choice to me. I say send the Contract back with your changes and wait to see what happens. My bet is they'll sweeten the deal, maybe agree to some of the things you've asked for, but not all. You can play it for a while, but sooner or later you're going to have to make a decision and if you wait too long, you might lose not only the Contract, but all your upcoming independent gigs as well. These guys don't fool around. They're in this for one reason: to make money. They don't care who they screw in the process because to them, it's all about choices."

"And on some level, it is," JayJay agreed. "We don't have to be musicians. We don't have to want to make a living at it. We can survive the way we are now, but it's almost as

if we've drawn too much attention to ourselves, put ourselves out in front and now we've got to play or get off stage."

"Yeah," Phoenix agreed, "you do."

※ ※ ※

In the early morning light, Michelle slept. Finally. She'd arrived home in a Studio car in the deepest part of the night. In the time when the darkness feels as though it will never end and the nightmares which accompany that darkness overwhelm the senses like fog suffocates a valley. Corlay, reading in a chair beneath a single lamp, had looked up when Michelle came from the shadowed room to the edge of the pool of light. It had taken Corlay a moment to let her eyes adjust, to see Michelle's bruised face, the coat clutched tightly around her, her legs in the synthetic jumpsuit sticking out below the coat's hem.

Corlay jumped up then. "What the hell?"

Michelle looked up at her, eyes moving rapidly back and forth across Corlay's face as if searching for something. She swallowed and her throat worked against tears. She opened her mouth, but found she could not make words come. She'd been holding the tatters of her emotions together for what seemed like years and a dam threatened to burst inside her. She wanted it to crumble, wanted in some growing part of her, to let Corlay come in and fill all the lonely places, but she found when the opportunity was there, she couldn't do it. Couldn't trust enough that, come morning, Corlay would still be here. So instead of speaking, she walked through the light's golden arc and into the shadows.

In the bathroom, she bent over the tub and let the water splash into the shining porcelain. Steam rose and

THE WHITE BONES OF TRUTH

covered the mirror. Rose like a veiling mist. She struggled with her coat and felt hands at her shoulder, whirled in confusion and fear, saw Corlay's face creased with concern, and crumpled finally into sobbing release.

Corlay undressed her carefully, eased her into the steaming water, watched it redden as blood leaked out from between Michelle's thighs. Sitting on the edge of the tub, stroking Michelle's hair, Corlay didn't have to use much imagination to put together the pieces of what had happened. She cried silently as Michelle stared blankly ahead, lost in the netherworld of numbness, the place she had retreated to for safety, for survival. Corlay knew that place and understood, as only another who has been the victim of such brutality and terror can, that only time and patience would allow Michelle to emerge again.

Careful of the darkening bruises, Corlay raised Michelle from the tub, wrapped her in a towel. "Did they give you anything for the pain?" Corlay asked.

"No. In the cabinet. There's some HCL. I want to sleep."

Corlay found the pink tablets. Prescription sleeping pills. She popped two from their blister packs and gave them to Michelle with some water. They moved like awkward dancers to the bedroom where Michelle donned her sleeping clothes as if in a trance. Corlay tucked the covers up around her and then took up her place in a chair beside the bed.

The sun was already cresting the edge of the world. It was another day. A new day. But nothing about it felt new. There was no promise of some shiny surprise which would thrill and delight, nothing except the dark bruises on a young woman's body and the nightmares flickering like loops of film behind her eyes.

※ ※ ※

JayJay was the only one awake when Phoenix departed. Sipping coffee in the kitchen, she looked up from her study of the Contract when he came in. "Water's still hot," she said.

He made himself coffee and sat down opposite her. "I have to go find Robert."

"You realize that isn't a very good idea. Even if he has been released, as you readily admitted, he's probably under house arrest. The place'll be crawling with some kind of private cop."

"Just because it's difficult doesn't mean I don't need to do it."

"Need or want?" she countered.

"Need. Next to Corlay, Robert's the most important person in my life."

"Is he your lover?"

Phoenix didn't answer right away. "We complete each other," he said at last. "Sometimes it's sexual, if that's what you mean."

"I guess."

"I've known him my whole life. I can't imagine being without him and I know he feels the same way about me. His parent, Rafael, and Corlay were ... similar. We kind of grew up together. It was a strange childhood, but a loving one. Robert's parent committed suicide five years ago, during the really nasty political campaign. Losing Rafael nearly killed Corlay. She hasn't been the same since."

"Your guardian is a ..." JayJay began.

"Yes. She is. She's a genetic experiment. A mutant, if you like." His voice was hard and he felt himself shutting

THE WHITE BONES OF TRUTH

down. "Do you have a problem with that?" he asked harshly, almost spoiling for a fight.

JayJay put her hand on his arm. "No. Calm down, will you? I don't have a problem with it. It's just a bit of a shock. Something you read about but never expect you'll encounter first hand, that's all." JayJay paused. "I don't feel disgusted, if that's what you mean."

"Yeah. I guess. My whole life has been about either hiding it or defending it. Every time I meet someone new, I have to decide whether or not I want to discuss who Corlay is. What she is. That's part of the reason why Robert is so important to me. I don't have to explain anything to him. He understands."

JayJay nodded. "Well, I'm glad you told me. I can't profess to understand what your life has been like, but I can say I've experienced some prejudice myself. In any form it's horrible and frustrating. It's hard to keep a clear sense of who you are when the world tells you you're bad or stupid or ugly. That the very fact of your being alive is somehow an affront to the rest of humanity. The 'normal' majority, whatever the hell that is."

"It's a lie," Phoenix said. "That's what it is. What's normal and who decides? If androgynes ruled the world, a lot of things would be abnormal."

JayJay laughed. "Yeah. But I think I'd rather live in that world. At least there'd be some real discussion about gender."

"Yeah," Phoenix agreed. "Sometimes I don't really think of myself as a man first and foremost. I think of myself as a human being and then all the other labels society has applied or I've adopted come into play. I'm a person first. That's what Corlay taught me. Someone of value and worth.

We all are. Gender defines us too much, I think," he said. "I wish people could get past it sometimes and just deal with each other on the level that really matters, where we're real to each other. Where we're pure."

"That'd be nice," JayJay said. Phoenix expected her to continue with a disclaimer. She didn't, though, and they sat together in silence for a few minutes.

"I should go," he said at last, rising from the table. He rinsed his mug out and set it beside the sink.

"Will you come back?"

"If it's safe for both of us, yes. Otherwise ..." he shrugged. "I really appreciate your hospitality. And your friendship."

JayJay rose from the table and embraced him. "You're welcome here anytime, friend." She walked him to the door then and watched him disappear down the shadowed hall, wondering when or if she'd ever see him again.

❅ ❅ ❅

Out on the street the hot July sun was already baking the asphalt. Phoenix walked swiftly to a local Tube station and inserted a Credit chip into the reader. He juggled five others in his hands. His supply was very low. Maybe Robert would be able to lend him some chips until he could manage to unfreeze his account. If he could get in touch with Corlay, he knew she could do it. He decided to send her a message from Robert's when he arrived.

Robert Hennigan's home was in one of the most exclusive and isolated sections of Bel Air. Access from the street was limited to the main entrance gate which had not only a card reader, but a guard station as well. As Phoenix

THE WHITE BONES OF TRUTH

suspected, it was occupied. Surveillance cameras positioned along the high stone walls swept the grounds constantly as well as the area along the outside wall.

Phoenix, approaching the mansion from the back, walked carefully in the shadows, keeping as close to the wall as possible. Although, ever since he could remember, Phoenix had had access through the front gate, there had been times when, breaking curfew, he'd snuck out or into the Hennigan estate by way of an oak tree at the southern edge of the property.

The estate, which had become Robert's upon Rafael's death, had been built nearly thirty years ago just after Rafael made his fortune in the Tokyo Stock Exchange. He'd retired to this place and continued to do consulting work out of his home until his death at the age of fifty. He'd been one of the first androgynes. The first generation of genetically engineered humans. Corlay, created twenty years after Rafael, had been part of the second generation. Robert was actually Rafael's nephew, a fact only the court system and the 'keepers knew for certain outside of a few close friends. Raffi had wanted to raise a child and his adopted sister had been willing to carry his seed.

Phoenix found the familiar tree and waited for the cameras to pan away. Then, in the seconds their electronic eyes were gazing elsewhere, he leapt from the ground and wrapped his arms around the lowest branch he could reach. Pulling himself up swiftly, he huddled amid the leaves until the way was clear again. Ten times he paused and waited. Finally he dropped down into the estate grounds and ran for the stable.

The internal estate phone line was still intact and Phoenix lifted the receiver knowing it would automatically ring on a private circuit. He waited anxiously for either the familiar voice or an unfamiliar one, finger poised above the disconnect key. "Hello?" It was Robert, sounding hesitant and confused.

"It's Phoenix," he whispered.

"Christ. Where are you?"

"The barn. Create a diversion."

"Give me five minutes," Robert said, and the line went dead.

Five minutes later the main gate alarm went off and Phoenix ran toward the main house. When he reached the back door, Robert was there. He ushered Phoenix quickly inside. "Upstairs. My old room." He pushed Phoenix in the direction of the staircase and then went out into the main hall.

Phoenix waited upstairs anxiously. He heard shouts and voices and then, after about twenty minutes had passed, Robert came into the room and closed the door behind him. The two men embraced eagerly, then kissed more gently. "It's so good to see you," Robert said.

"Are you all right?" Phoenix asked.

Robert nodded. "House arrest until further notice. You?"

"I was followed to Corlay's. The 'keepers broke into the apartment. I got out through one of the old chutes and ended up in the warehouse district."

"Really?"

Phoenix filled him in on the details and then asked if he could use the Net terminal to send a message to Corlay.

"Sure," Robert said. He gestured to the terminal sitting on a nearby desk.

"Before I do, I need you to promise me something."

"Anything. What?"

THE WHITE BONES OF TRUTH

"You set off the proximity alarm out front, didn't you?"

Robert grinned. "The remote still works."

"Yeah, but since you're under house arrest they're going to be looking for someone on the premises. If they find me, say it was a break-in, okay? Don't put yourself in danger."

"Phoenix, that's crazy."

"No," he insisted. "It's not. They'll just take me downtown. You refuse to press charges. I'll be inside seventy-two hours, tops. You've got to do this, Robert. Otherwise who knows what the hell The Studio will do. And I don't want to read about your untimely death in the papers."

Robert crossed the room and stood beside Phoenix. "I don't want to do this."

"I know. But you trust me, don't you?"

"Of course I do."

"Then promise."

"All right," Robert said at last. "I promise." Phoenix sat down in front of the Net terminal and typed on the keyboard. He didn't need to go virtual — e-mail would work just fine. Robert could delete everything later. When the green circle in the upper right hand corner of the screen flashed, indicating he could begin sending, he began to speak.

Suddenly there was a banging on the suite's outer door. Robert glanced once at Phoenix, then closed the bedroom door behind him as he left. Phoenix, hearing voices in the outer room, rose as the door to the bedroom slammed open. His fingers fumbled then found the disconnect key just as two guards barrelled into the room.

Robert stood behind them. "I'm so glad you came

up," he said, his voice trembling. "I just didn't know what to do."

"Do you know this man?" one of the guards asked.

"No. I've never seen him before." Robert waved his hand. "Probably some deranged fan."

The guard looked at Robert as if trying to decide whether or not to believe him. Then he gestured to Phoenix. "Turn around and put your hands on the desk. You're under arrest." As the guard ushered him out, Phoenix half-turned and saw Robert's tear-streaked face.

✢ ✢ ✢

When The Studio called, Corlay was jolted out of an uneasy doze. For a moment she debated about answering the call, but in the end punched the connect button and dimmed the screen so the caller could not see her face. "This is Justin Mitchell from The Studio's legal department," the man on the other end of the line said. "Who are you?"

"A friend of Michelle's. She called me last night when she got in."

"Then you've heard what happened."

"She wasn't very talkative."

Justin shrugged. It was clear he wasn't going to elaborate but was just fishing for information. "I need to speak with Michelle."

"She's sleeping right now. Leave a message with me and I'll see she gets it."

Mitchell frowned. "Turn on the recording feature," he directed. Corlay complied and he began speaking as if she were not there. "This is Justin Mitchell. It's 7:30 on Thursday, July 28. The Studio has authorized a four-day

vacation. You are to report for work on Monday, August 1, no later than 8:00 a.m. in studio 41-B. Shooting will begin at 10:00. You might want to allow a little extra time for makeup that day. We'll be faxing you some paperwork later today." He reached toward the screen and severed the connection. Corlay watched Mitchell's image fade. Then she turned away and went back into the bedroom to wait.

It was early afternoon before Michelle awoke. She rose silently from the wide bed, careful not to wake Corlay, who had fallen asleep again in the chair, and went into the bathroom. Deliberately not looking in the mirror, she relieved herself, brushed her teeth and then returned to the bedroom. A thin strip of light from where the curtains were parted cut across Corlay's face. In sleep, her features were softened, almost childlike. Looking at her then, Michelle felt so grateful for Corlay's undemanding, comforting presence that she almost cried. She couldn't remember the last time she'd woken at home and felt safe in the presence of another person.

Michelle sat on the edge of the bed next to the chair and touched Corlay's hand. The dark eyes opened slowly and Michelle watched as Corlay seemed to drop into herself from the place where dreams are made. Corlay smiled and straightened in the chair. Then grimaced. "It looks more comfortable than it is," she said with a chuckle.

"Why didn't you sleep in the bed?"

"I was afraid you'd wake up and be frightened to find someone beside you. Especially a stranger."

"You're not a stranger, Corlay."

The other shrugged. "How are you?"

Michelle shook her head. "I feel ... like every inch of my body is bruised." She looked down at her hands. "But mostly I feel cheap."

Corlay got up and sat beside Michelle on the bed. "You're not. You're a human being caught in a dehumanizing situation. It's not your fault."

"But it is. I signed the Contract, Corlay. No one held a gun to my head. I wanted the life I thought they were offering me — glamour, money, a chance to meet people who didn't have to get their hands dirty to make a living. But what I got is a life without morality, without kindness."

"We're all struggling to find a way to live with dignity in these times. This is the bottom, Michelle. You have nowhere to go but up."

"No," Michelle's head came up swiftly. "I have nowhere to go. This isn't an unusual occurrence, Corlay. It's happened before, just not this badly. The Studio is supposed to screen its clients. How this one got through, I don't know. But I've been hurt before. And every time I have to lie beneath some stranger, the hidden wounds get deeper.

"What if I did just walk away?" she mused, then shook her head. "I can't. They'd find me. I owe them so much money now that even if my next three films break all known records, I still won't be out of the hole."

"Why is that? Can't you control your expenses? Live in a cheaper part of town?"

Michelle shook her head. "The Contract requires we live in certain areas, shop at certain stores ... and then those merchants can raise their prices as much as they want."

"But doesn't the Studio lose money that way?"

"At a five-hundred percent markup? No. It's just a paper game, the huge Credit debts. Both the Studio and the merchants are making more than they know what to do with. The only ones who suffer are those of us caught in the middle."

"What if you go outside the Studio and get a loan?"

"Tried it. No bank will take a risk on someone who will lose her job the moment the loan is discovered. And the creditors who work outside the law ... their payback rate is just not realistic. I don't want to end up in some gutter with my throat cut because I can't pay them back fast enough." Michelle pushed herself off the bed and paced with angry, nervous energy. "I've been through all this before, Corlay. There isn't one option I haven't tried. I spent a year trying to break Contract legally, using all my personal allotment money to pay outside legal council. The document is ironclad. Once you're in, it's for life. And then if you die in debt, they go after your families, your children. My family legally disowned me five years ago. They can't even afford to be seen with me." She turned and faced Corlay, "It'll happen to you, too, Corlay. You put yourself in danger just being here."

"I'm not afraid of whatever The Studio thinks it can do."

"You're not afraid of death? Accidents have been known to happen, especially when outsiders —"

"—I am not afraid of death, Michelle," Corlay broke in. "Death and I are old companions. We have met on this road many times. And I have learned the risks I take, whether with Phoenix or with you or with any other person I come to care for, are worth — for me — the consequences. We are not made to be without love, without companionship. Loneliness will kill you just as surely as an assassin's gun. I'm not afraid to be here, if you are not afraid to have me."

Michelle came to the bed and sat down again. She took Corlay's hands in her own, felt strength there, looked into her eyes and saw love. At first it startled her, then it frightened her. She'd seen what she thought was love before and it had always turned out to be something else. Could she take a chance that this person would be different? That Corlay's feelings for her, whatever they were, were as simple and clearcut as they seemed?

She had made no demands, asked for no favors. She had only agreed to accompany Michelle back to her apartment after being pressed and there had been no coyness in that conversation. And she had refused to make love with Michelle, something no one had ever done before. That, more than anything else, stayed in her mind.

Michelle dropped her eyes to where her hands enclosed Corlay's. Pale marble against mahogany; she liked the contrast. She could not imagine these hands hurting her any more than she could imagine Corlay acting in a manner which was intentionally cruel. She looked up at Corlay again, trying to put her thoughts into words.

But before she could, Corlay said, "I'm not asking you to make any kind of a commitment to me, Michelle. If that's what you're thinking. And if you want me to go home now, I will. I would have left last night but I was worried about you and—"

"I don't really know what I want other than I don't want you to go."

"That's enough," Corlay said. "All you need to know about is right now." Michelle nodded. Corlay started to rise from the bed, but Michelle put out a hand to stop her. "Hold me," she said. "Just for a while."

Corlay opened her arms, felt warmth spread through her as Michelle slipped into them and knew that even though she could not bear to speak it aloud for fear of seeing even the slightest hesitation in Michelle's face or hear the catch in

THE WHITE BONES OF TRUTH

her voice, she loved this woman and before she died, would tell her just how much.

In the late afternoon, Michelle read Justin Mitchell's message. Corlay had gone out for a while, but had promised to return before dark. While she was sorting through the rest of her e-mail, a fax came through from the Studio. She ripped it from the machine and glanced down. What she saw brought a flash of anger and then despair. Fifty-two thousand Credits: ten thousand Credits, charged to her account for refusing to press charges against her rapist. Two thousand Credits for bail. And forty thousand Credits for the loss of work time due to an injury suffered while not on Studio property. These charges, coupled with her already enormous debt, sealed her fate. There was no escaping this ever-deepening hole. No escape but death. But her mind turned away from that idea, choice or no. She had been raised to think of life as precious, not to be taken or lived lightly. And she had tried to live that way. What, then, had she done so wrong to be punished in this way?

The fax fell out of numb fingers and for a long time she sat staring at the computer screen without seeing it. That was how Corlay found her several hours later when she returned with dinner and more bad news.

✢ ✢ ✢

The streets outside Michelle's apartment building were wide and kept clean of debris. Unmarked Peacekeeper cars patrolled at regular intervals and the gardens and trees were all well tended. Corlay boarded the Tube at the closest station and took it to the main Market Square where a week from tomorrow, California's Independence Day would be celebrated with a three-day Festival beginning on Friday evening, August fifth, with a live concert and continuing non-stop until Sunday afternoon.

California had its own holidays and Festival was, aside from the shopping frenzy that was still associated with the winter Christmas celebration, the biggest event of the year. As she approached the Net terminal that had been her designated rendezvous spot with Phoenix for ten years, she wondered whether or not he was planning on attending Festival, or if he'd even be able to.

Like the Mardi Gras still celebrated in the segregated South and in other cultures around the world, Festival was a three-day reprieve from the structures of daily life. A time for cross-dressing, drunkenness and illicit sex in public places, it was a safety valve for an uptight society. For Corlay, it had always been a time to hide in the open, to walk in whichever shape suited her and entertain fantasies she never acted upon. It was a time to partake in the sensual pleasures of food and drink. To tease a young man or woman in the crowd with her eyes. To flirt without fear of recrimination. To pretend she was just like everyone else. To feel a part of the society which otherwise despised her.

Today the Market Square was bustling with the normal daily activity of an open-air market in a busy city. Merchants' stalls hawking everything from fresh produce to jewelry to bolts of cloth to pottery formed arbitrary streets within the square itself. Hundreds of people jostled, shouted and bartered at the various tables under bright canopies flapping in the dry wind.

Peacekeepers walked among the crowd, their gunmetal helmets flashing in the burning sun, looking like some sort of alien bugs in contrast to the casually dressed

THE WHITE BONES OF TRUTH

shoppers and merchants. No vehicles were allowed on the Square between the hours of eight a.m. and ten p.m. After that, merchants were allowed to bring trucks onto the pavilion to store their wares. And since the square was patrolled all night by both private and public forces, merchants often left locked trucks parked next to their stalls overnight.

Corlay moved easily through the crowd and headed for a series of boxes attached to a nearby bank. These were public Net terminals, each encased in a smoke-grey box for privacy. The second box on the left was the terminal she and Phoenix had used over the years when it was too dangerous to be in touch directly. The last time had been nearly five years ago during a particularly gruesome election campaign in which one of the candidates called for the elimination of everyone he considered a sexual pervert. Androgynes, naturally, were high on his list and Corlay's house had been bugged and monitored for months. She grimaced, thinking of that time, but then had to smile when she remembered that particular candidate had bowed out of the race quite unexpectedly when someone discovered he had a real penchant for the S/M call-in lines. The tapes, she remembered, had been comic at best for her and humiliating for him. And she wondered why people bothered to run for office on such a volatile platform if they kept such dangerous skeletons in their closets. Someone always found out.

Inside the box, Corlay slipped on the VR glove and headpiece. Using a back door into the system, she walked the virtual corridor until she found the private bulletin board she was looking for. Not only was the board itself hidden from the casual observer by a series of codes, but the message itself was encrypted. Only someone who knew them well could even begin to guess at the passwords. And even if someone did manage to break into the message, there was an autodestruct sequence which would initiate five seconds after the message was retrieved unless a final password was entered.

Phoenix had often said he thought the elaborate system was a bit much, but Corlay had insisted. And now she was glad she had. Now, privacy really mattered. She entered the last of the passwords and a moment later the message appeared on the screen.

It was Phoenix, standing close to a screen in a house Corlay didn't recognize and speaking rapidly. "I'm okay. Found some friends I didn't know I had. Meet me at the old spot the first evening of Festival. Lots to—-" then chaos erupted behind him. A door was flung open and several 'keepers stormed into the room. Phoenix turned, his hand reaching for the screen and the message was severed. A single line of type scrolled across the now black terminal: *Transmission Incomplete. 28 July '54. 14:21. Transmission Origin Unknown.* Corlay cleared the screen and took a deep breath to steady herself. Earlier that day. It appeared as though he'd been arrested again.

For a moment she sat in silence, then she wiggled her fingers again and went back into the Net. Her icon, the black-garbed harpist, strode through several corridors and stopped at an information node to get directions. Accessing the directory, she watched a series of addresses scroll by until the one she wanted, or at least the one closest to her real destination, appeared on the screen. Then she turned, got her bearings in a world in which there were no real directions, and headed for the central file system at Peacekeeper Headquarters.

THE WHITE BONES OF TRUTH

Once there, she knew she wouldn't have much time. In fact, she would have only one shot at breaking into their prisoner list before the system would alert its users and the watchdogs would descend. So standing before the imposing steel door which was supposed to discourage all hackers, she stilled her mind and tried to imagine where the data might be stored. Then, slipping a tool from her hip-pouch, she slid it into the space between the door and the frame and lifted her arm up. There was a click and she was in.

Corlay figured she had about thirty seconds to find the file and she scanned the huge file drawers which filled the space before her, looking for something that would contain the prisoners' list. There. She pulled the drawer open and pulled the file out. Ten seconds left.

At the bottom of the list she saw Phoenix's name. Just then an alarm went off and she spun, momentarily dizzy from the disorientation of the virtual world. The door was beginning to close. Running, she scrambled to bridge the distance and managed to squeeze through just before the door slammed shut.

But it wasn't over yet. She could hear the yapping of the 'keepers' watchdogs growing louder. If they caught her, her identity would be revealed to 'keeper system security and she'd most likely be arrested herself. Just then a voice called, "Deth! Deth, this way."

She turned and saw the shimmer of the little rainstorm. She ran, ducking behind the curtain of virtual rain just before the watchdogs entered that section of corridor. She felt someone tug at her hand and felt herself pulled through an unfamiliar access node, out of the main Net corridor and into a dark and seedy bar.

"What?" the Deth icon said, looking around.

"It's Barleyman Butterburr's tavern," the shimmer said and Deth laughed aloud. "I do read, you know," the shimmer continued.

"So you do." The shimmer changed into an icon of a kind of generic female elf — tall and slender with pointed ears and silver hair. "What shall I call you, friend?"

"Just Elf will do."

"You prefer your anonymity?" Deth asked.

"I do. And if I remember correctly, you are the one who cautioned me to be careful." She moved to the bar and ordered two tankards of ale. A fat barkeep with sweat standing out on his brow delivered them, muttering to himself and took her coins absently. Elf gestured to a secluded table and they sat down together.

"What were you doing in the 'keeper's files?" Elf asked.

Deth didn't answer for a long time and then she said, "Are you offering to trade information?"

Elf looked surprised. "It was just a question."

"But a question whose answer would reveal much. So I ask again — are you offering a trade?"

"Yes," Elf answered without hesitation. "I am."

"Give me something first," Deth said. "To show your good intentions."

"I read your notice on the bulletin board," Elf began. "The one you posted the other night while your harp was playing to distract me. I know the access code you need. I'll give it to you in exchange for the reason you were in the 'keeper's files."

Deth hesitated. She felt she was getting the better part of the deal and thought for a time about whether there was a hidden agenda she had not yet uncovered. Finally she

said, "All right. And to show my good faith, I'll go first." She paused and sipped at the ale to buy time. The elf's eyes did not leave her face. "I was looking for my son. I think he was arrested earlier today and I was trying to find out where he was being held and whether or not his bail had been paid."

"And who is your son?" Elf asked.

"Give me the password first," Deth countered.

"*Oscar*."

"*Oscar?*" Deth sounded surprised.

"Yes. It was some kind of award the flickers used to give each other."

"And this will get me in?"

The elf nodded. "I swear it. Now, your son's name."

"Phoenix," Deth said. "Phoenix Whitson."

The elf looked visibly startled, and Deth leaned forward and gripped the other's arm. "You know him, don't you?"

"Yes," Elf said after a moment. "Yes. I do. He was staying with us. He left this morning." Deth let go of the elf's arm and leaned back in her chair. She didn't say anything for a long time. "Are you his guardian?" Elf asked.

"I have told you enough already," Deth replied. "There is nothing more I need and I do not wish to barter any longer." Deth stood up.

"Wait," the elf said. "I think we are about the same purpose here. Perhaps we should pool our resources."

"Perhaps. But there are other concerns which must come first." Deth strode toward the door and the elf hurried to follow. "Show me a safe way back to the corridor," she demanded in a voice that left no room for disagreement.

The elf nodded and extended her right hand. She drew a square in the air before her and spoke a word. A

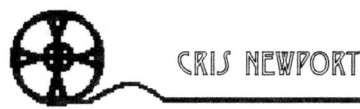

doorway appeared. Deth could see the corridor beyond it. She turned. This elf was a better surfer than she had first imagined.

"My thanks," Deth said. Then she stepped through the doorway and was gone.

✽ ✽ ✽

At Peacekeeper Central, a woman introducing herself as Street Captain Madeline Mahoney looked from Corlay's ID card to the woman standing before her. With an unreadable expression, she handed the card back to Corlay and touched the screen in front of her. Corlay saw it flicker to life and reflect in the shiny material of her suit. Mahoney frowned in concentration and then said, "Sorry, no one of that name or description has been processed through this center in the last twenty-four hours."

Corlay felt fury course through her. She knew the Captain was lying, but was in no position to prove it. Gritting her teeth, Corlay nodded. She didn't ask the Captain to double check. She knew the results would not change and didn't want to give the other any more reason to remember her than she already had. Corlay thanked the Captain and left. Madeline stared after her, pursing her lips. Then she accessed Phoenix's file and made a note that someone had tried to post bail for the young man who "officially" did not exist in the computer's records.

By the time Corlay returned again to Michelle's apartment, she was exhausted and discouraged. Balancing a bag of take-out food on her hip, she slid the pass Michelle had loaned her through the card reader and entered the spacious lobby.

THE WHITE BONES OF TRUTH

She found Michelle where she'd left her, sitting before the Net terminal, staring blankly ahead. Corlay set the food down on the dining room table and went to Michelle's side. The actress looked up and smiled wanly. Corlay picked up the fax from where it had fallen to the floor. "Christ," she said.

"I can't do this anymore," Michelle said thickly.

"I know." Corlay rose from where she'd been squatting on the floor and lifted Michelle out of the chair. "Come eat."

"I'm not hungry."

"Eat anyway. We have some decisions to make."

They left the apartment separately several hours later, meeting up again as if by accident at the Tube station. From there they headed to the warehouse district, riding in silence through the encased tunnel, watching their reflections flicker against the darkened window, hands wrapped around soft carrybags containing all they hoped they might need to make a new start underground. The Studio wouldn't begin looking for Michelle in earnest until Monday and it was only Thursday night. And Corlay knew there was nothing she could do for Phoenix now, no way to get him from the bowels of Central where she was convinced he was being held. Another political prisoner. She prayed for strength, prayed someone would free him — be it the Whitsons or some other generous soul — and tried not to blame herself for not being able to do more.

Michelle's hand brushed Corlay's and they exchanged a fleeting smile. Then they had arrived and departed the train at a poorly lit station. "Are you sure you know where this place is?" Corlay asked.

Michelle nodded. "I did some checking. It's about five

blocks from here." She started out and Corlay fell into step beside her. The wide streets were windblown and piles of trash huddled in corners as if trying to escape notice. The evening sky was nearly dark now but there were no stars. Instead, a pale orange glow pulsed against the deeper blackness beyond. City lights. The heartbeat of the urban animal.

Harsh light shone down upon them as they moved from shadow to light to shadow again. The warehouse facades were covered with graffiti, but the streets were deserted. Finally, after several long blocks, Michelle stopped and gestured. There, several storeys above the street, was a lit series of square windows and in the upper left corner of one were three black bandannas. "That's the one," she said.

They crossed the street and pushed open the heavy steel door. A painted red arrow pointed upward and someone had scrawled *Bandshees* in black marker on the wall above it. At the top of the stairs, they came to another door illuminated by a bare light bulb suspended from a wire above them. To the left of the door was a metal tray with an electronic lock embedded into the wall and a button above it. In black marker someone had written: *Ring for Service*. Michelle pushed the button, heard a buzzer sound somewhere within. After a few moments they heard footsteps and a woman's voice, distorted by a speaker, called out, "Yeah? What do you want?"

"I've come to see JayJay," Michelle said. "Is she there?"

"Who wants to know?"

"Michelle David," she said.

There was a long silence. "Put your ID in the drawer."

THE WHITE BONES OF TRUTH

"Put yours in first," Michelle countered.

There was short bark of laughter. "You got a lot of balls, lady. See the camera above your head? Hold up your ID."

Michelle did. A minute later the heavy steel door slid to the right and Michelle and JayJay set eyes on each other for the first time. "If you were men, I wouldn't do this," she said. "Come in." Corlay and Michelle stepped inside and the heavy door clanged shut behind them.

They followed JayJay into the run-down living room and took a seat together on the couch. JayJay held out her hand. "Your ID," she said. Michelle handed it to her. JayJay looked at it then handed it back. From around her neck she took a chain. Her ID dangled on the end of it and she handed it to Michelle. "Who's your friend?"

"This is Corlay Llewellyn, the painter."

"Never heard of you."

Corlay smiled. "I'm not that well known."

"Not Contracted, eh?"

Corlay shook her head. "No. Don't believe in them."

"Lucky you. To have those kind of options. Looks like you make a decent living."

"I did. Once." Corlay felt tired suddenly. Tired of the games. The tests. "I know who you are and, although you don't realize it, you also know me."

"What the fuck are you talking about?" JayJay asked. Corlay could feel the woman's fear.

She took a deep breath before she continued. "I've met you on the Net, Elf," she said. "There I am known as Deth, the High One's harpist."

JayJay drew in a sharp breath. "Phoenix's guardian."

Corlay nodded. There was no point in hiding that

now. "We have much to discuss, I think, the three of us. You trusted me once and I trusted you."

"I saved your ass," JayJay admonished.

Corlay smiled. "True. So, can we skip the posturing and get down to business?"

"Yeah," JayJay said. "Sure."

"How was my son," Corlay asked. "the last time you saw him?"

"Fine. He came up through some kind of tunnel into our practice room. He was here for a day or so. He left this morning to find his friend, Robert."

Several things suddenly made sense to Corlay and she nodded. The transmission must have come from Robert's, then, and not this place.

"Were you able to find out if he'd been arrested?" JayJay asked.

"He has," Corlay responded. "But when I went down to Central to post his bail, the Captain on duty claimed no one fitting that description with that name had been processed."

"That's bullshit," JayJay snarled.

"Yes. And I will get him out. I'm just not sure how I'll do it."

JayJay cursed. She flopped down into a chair opposite the couch. "I was afraid something like this would happen. I tried to tell him to stay here." For a long moment the room was quiet. Then JayJay said to Michelle, "I guess you got our message."

Michelle nodded. "As of Monday morning I'll be breaking Contract."

"Why did you come here?" JayJay asked, suddenly suspicious.

THE WHITE BONES OF TRUTH

"I don't expect you to harbor us, if that's what you're thinking. I want to tell you the truth. Maybe you can do something about it. I don't think I can."

"And you?" JayJay said to Corlay.

"I am here to help you. You're up to something. I've been watching you for months. I have a plan as well. It seemed the time was right to pool our resources."

"As opposed to this afternoon."

"My son was my only concern this afternoon," Corlay said evenly.

JayJay just swallowed and nodded, thinking she didn't want to be on this one's bad side. "Okay," she said finally. "Let's pool. I'm listening. And I've got all night."

They were deep in conversation when Alejandro came into the living room several hours later. After introductions were concluded, JayJay said to him, "So tell me everything."

Alejandro sighed. "Sam agreed with your suggestion. To send the Contract back with our changes. So that's what I did. I also got Danny-o and Kay to agree to wait and see what Oilslick's response will be although I don't know how long I'll be able to stall those two. They're both much more willing to take the risk than either of us."

"Don't let Danny-o sway you, Alejandro," JayJay said earnestly. "After what I've heard tonight, there's no way I'm signing anything that even remotely resembles a Contract and if you sign, I'll have to."

"What do you mean?" Corlay asked.

"We're a group. But legally Kay and I have no rights," JayJay explained. "When we signed with the Independent label two years ago, Kay and I had to agree to stay with the group until the time the band called it quits. Danny-o and

Alejandro are free to leave at any time — they're men — but I can't. So if Alejandro agrees to sign, since Danny-o already wants to, I won't have any choice."

He reached for JayJay's hand. "I won't do anything without consulting you first."

"I know. But somehow that doesn't convince me you won't do what you think is best for all of us, even if it means signing the Contract. Even if that's not what I want."

"What do you want then, JayJay?"

"I want whatever freedom I can have. I want to be free to make my own decisions about what lyrics I write and what arrangements I make for the band. I want to be free to come and go as I please, to live where I like and see who I choose. We risk losing all that if we sign."

"But we gain so much," Alejandro persisted.

"No," Michelle said. "You gain nothing. Please reconsider. Don't sign anything."

"And then what? Stay as we are living here on the cutting edge of poverty? What kind of a life is that for us? We have an opportunity to do something—"

"—they will silence you," Michelle cut in suddenly, her voice harsh. "Haven't you ever noticed that once a band signs with a major label, all the fire goes out of their music? It's just provocative enough to be mildly entertaining, but the real risks have always been taken by those on the fringe. People like you. Doing what you're doing right now. Give up that freedom and you lose everything money can't buy — respect, honesty, self-honor."

"This from a Contracted Star?"

"I was a fool—"

"—how do we know you're not just a plant?" Alejandro countered, angry now. "Why should we trust

THE WHITE BONES OF TRUTH

you?"

Michelle stood up suddenly and, before Corlay could stop her, pulled her sweater over her head. Her torso was a mass of dark bruises and there were marks at her throat and wrists as well. "I got these last night entertaining a client. I was raped last night in a Studio-sanctioned after-hours meeting which I was required to participate in." Alejandro stared at her in horror, then turned his eyes away. "You're an attractive man, Alejandro. How long do you think it's going to be before Oilslick starts asking you to entertain guests in return for extra studio time, a little more control over your music? You want to lie on your face while some man shoves his dick up your ass? Is that the kind of life you want? You want JayJay to know you're out fucking some bitch while she sits home waiting for you? How long do you think your relationship's going to last, man? How long do you think she's going to wait for you to come home from your whoring? How long until she starts resenting you? Hating you? You want to lose her? Fine. Sign the damned thing. You want to end up like me? Look like this? Fine. Sign your fucking life away. But don't say I didn't warn you." She turned away then, furious, and snatched the sweater out of Corlay's hands. Storming from the room, she slammed the door to the only bathroom. The walls shook and then there was a long silence.

"She took a big risk to come here," JayJay said gently. Alejandro wouldn't look at her. "I believe her. I don't want to live like that, baby. I can't."

He looked up at her then, his face full of shame and his eyes brimming with unshed tears. "I'm sorry," he murmured. JayJay went to him, cradled his head against her breasts. His arms went around her. "But what are we going

to do?" he asked again and again. "What are we going to do?"

Corlay got up, leaving the two lovers comforting each other and knocked on the bathroom door. Michelle opened it at the sound of Corlay's voice and stepped into the narrow hallway. "Maybe it was mistake to come here," Michelle said.

"No. You got through to him."

Michelle looked up at Corlay. In the dim reflected light from the bathroom, she could only make out the sharp planes and hollows of Corlay's face. The distinctly androgynous features looked at times more feminine and at times wholly masculine. Corlay was a continuing unfolding mystery to her, and she was hungry to know more. She reached up then and laid her hand against Corlay's cheek, slid her fingers across the warm skin to cup the back of Corlay's neck. Michelle tugged gently and Corlay bent her head, allowed Michelle's mouth to find hers. She tastes sweet, like chocolate, Michelle thought, losing herself in the sensation. She felt Corlay's body move closer. Felt Corlay's hands lift to cup her face, felt breath warm on her cheek, felt a radiating warmth like sun-warmed honey flow through her. She pushed closer, wanting to crawl inside this other person, to feel enclosed in this soothing warmth.

A sound in the hallway distracted her. A cough and the scrape of a boot across the floor. She drew back reluctantly, felt Corlay melt into shadow beside her.

"Sorry to interrupt," JayJay said. "But Alejandro has an idea."

✾ ✾ ✾

CHAPTER 5
STATE OF INDEPENDENCE

CHAPTER FIVE: STATE OF INDEPENDENCE

When Monday the first of August dawned, Danny-o rolled over and groaned. The sky was still pearled white and he'd only been asleep for a few hours. Then the realization of what day this was hit him and he sat up in his soiled bed. Today was the day he had to make a decision about whether to stay with the band or give it up.

For a long moment, he just lay staring at the ceiling, a thin sheet stretched across his sweat-grimed body. Kay slept on, oblivious to his torment, on a pallet of her own in the room's opposite corner. He swung his legs over the edge of the bed finally and pulled on some clothes. Five minutes later he was gone.

Across town in the Peacekeeper's Central Office, Street Captain Madeline Mahoney was just about to get off duty. She walked down the long corridor of holding cells, noting many of them were now empty. Another weekend was over. But one cell still held its occupant. One Phoenix Whitson. His single Net access had left him cursing. That had been Thursday night. Since then he'd spoken to no one, just lay on his bunk, staring at the ceiling.

She stopped at the cell's door. "When's somebody going to post your bail, boy? You aren't cut out for this sort of life," she jeered, knowing full well someone had indeed tried to post his bail and the Unit Commander had deliberately ordered the record deleted. But Madeline had been there. She remembered the androgyne who'd come looking for the young man. Someone cared about what happened to him.

She wasn't sure why this particular prisoner hadn't been released yesterday. Robert Hennigan, whose house the Whitson kid had broken into, had refused to press charges. There was no reason to hold him. No reason other than his name was on The List.

But so what, she thought, standing on freedom's side of the prison bars. There were thousands on that list. For hundreds of different reasons. This one had been at a rally at The Studio demanding change. Him and five hundred others. Why were they holding him? She tried to puzzle out the Unit Commander's reasoning, but came up with nothing.

"You can't hold me more than seventy-two hours without formal charges. You're sixteen hours over," the young man said, breaking into her thoughts.

"And who's going to care?"

"You will when I haul your ass into court for failure to follow procedure. You'll be kicked off the force."

Madeline laughed. "You got to prove it first."

He turned his head toward her then and smiled grimly. "Oh, I can prove it, Street Captain," he said in a voice that made the hair on the back of her neck rise up. "And losing your job will be the least of your worries."

"Listen, punk," she spat, calling up more bravado than she felt, "just remember who's inside and who's outside."

"Yeah," he echoed. "Just remember." Then he looked away and resumed his study of the ceiling tiles.

Madeline didn't move, but continued to look at him. Then she said, "Why do you think you're still here?"

He spoke to the ceiling, "Because you have too much

THE WHITE BONES OF TRUTH

muscle and not enough grey matter between your ears. Hennigan didn't press charges. You have no reason and no right to hold me." He sat up suddenly and turned to face her. "What do you think I can tell you? What do you think I know?" He jumped down from the bunk and moved swiftly toward the bars.

Madeline took a step back, hand going to her electric prod, sarcastically called a joy stick, which she kept with her in the bowels of the prison cells.

"I'm calling your bluff, Captain. Tell me what you think I know and I'll tell you if you're right or not. But mark me, when I get out of here, I'll kick your ass all the way down Market Street."

"You know too much for your own good," she snarled, but she was intrigued. "They'll bury you in red tape, boy."

He laughed. "I've got a big pair of scissors."

They stood there for a moment with tension and curiosity crackling the air between them. Madeline relaxed first and put the joy stick back in its holder at her side. "I don't know why you're being held," she said, testing his reaction. His eyes widened and she knew she'd caught him off guard. "We've been forbidden to release you. No explanation."

Phoenix cursed and turned away. He paced the length of the cell then asked, "Did anyone try to post bail?"

Madeline nodded. "Corlay Llewellyn."

"So she knows I'm here."

"No. She doesn't. I was not permitted to confirm your arrest."

"You saw her?"

"You're related to that ... person?"

Phoenix, reacting to her hesitation, spat, "You look it up. You've probably got access to every fucking record available."

"Watch your mouth, boy."

He shot her a look of pure contempt. "Please, Captain. I'm not a boy and I'll use what ever fucking language I want. You just want me to tell you something. Well, guess what? I have nothing to tell you. I don't know why they're holding me. I'm just a driver for a warehouse across town. Don't know anyone. Don't know nothing. Until a few weeks ago, I didn't have one byte of info about me on the damned Net."

"You must have something they're after."

Phoenix shrugged. Then he shook his head and turned away. He wrapped his hands around the greasy bars, his face in profile in the harsh light. "You like your life, Captain?" he asked after a moment.

"It is what it is. I like what I do. In fact, I love it."

"The power? You get off on that?"

"No. Not like you mean. I got into this because I believed in the law."

He laughed harshly. "Not too gullible, are you?"

Madeline bristled then chastised herself. It was her own damn fault. If she hadn't wanted to hear his opinion, she never should have opened this avenue of conversation. "I guess I was, yes. I was idealistic. Just like you are."

He turned toward her then. "What do you mean?"

"You were at a protest at The Studio. Against Contracts. Considering how long they've been around and how prevalent they are and how people continue to sign them even though they're supposed to be so bad ... I'd say trying to change that system is like charging at windmills."

He grunted. The allusion of the mad knight errant was not lost on him. "So I have dreams of a better world. So what?"

"And you think I don't?"

"I don't know what you dream, Captain."

"You know Robert Hennigan, don't you? That wasn't B and E. It was all planned." Phoenix didn't respond. He just stared at her. "You work at Intercity Transport, right?" Again silence. "According to the records, you do. And according to our records, Mr. Gabriel Bell has quite a lengthy history with the department. If I were to hazard a guess, I'd say that's why you're being held. The Unit Commander wants to bleed you for information concerning Bell's current plans.

"He's a very effective interrogator, you know. Learned a lot by watching black market tapes." She leaned close to the bars. "Tapes of illegal interrogations in the other Americas. Where civil rights are not so ... prevalent?" She raised her eyebrows suggestively. He was sweating now and his pupils had dilated. She was scaring him. Good, she thought. Let him tremble a little in those self-righteous boots.

He didn't move or speak. She had to admire his ability to project his bravado, even though she could see right through it. "You want things to change, don't you?" she asked finally, softly.

"Of course I do. Anyone with any sense at all can see the system needs to be changed."

"Would it surprise you to know I want to see change as well?"

He looked hard at her then said, "Yes. I guess it would."

"The reasons I joined the Peacekeepers hasn't changed. But the force has. The society has. I'm powerless to

make change happen. In fact, more than any other group, I am expected to uphold the status quo."

Phoenix continued to stare at her. "If you're powerless to do something, then get out of the way."

"You're referring to yourself, I suppose," she said with feigned nonchalance.

"Captain." His voice was harsh, almost pleading, "I don't know what's going to happen. I don't know about plans or schemes. I only know that, like you, I can read the signs. Something is going to happen. And it will be soon. What will occur and when is beyond my knowledge. But change will come. Your Unit Commander has a better chance of killing me than getting information from me. I'm a driver, Captain. Nothing more."

"But you would like to be something more."

He laughed. "Wouldn't we all like to be something more than what we are?"

She sighed and nodded in agreement.

"Let me go," he said into the silence. "You can't hold me much longer anyway."

Her head came up and their eyes blazed into each other's. "Oh, but we can. We can twist the laws and alter the data in ways you can't imagine. We can bury you so deep within the system no one will ever find you."

"But what purpose would that serve?" he practically shouted. "Why punish me for ignorance?"

"Why release you to revolution?"

"Why not?" he countered. "Why the hell not? Let me do what you can't."

"What I won't."

"No," he said evenly. "What you can't."

She looked away. After a moment she shifted her

THE WHITE BONES OF TRUTH

weight and met his eyes again. "No promises," she said and walked away.

Upstairs the day Captain was signing in. He was just about to sit down at the terminal when she came into the small glass-encased office on the main floor. "Hey, Ricardo," she said, walking swiftly toward him. "Is it that time already?"

"Madeline," he returned, sitting down.

"Been upstairs yet?" she asked, her mind racing. She had to get access to the terminal before he logged himself into the Net for the day.

"No. Why?"

"The Unit Commander wanted to see you before you started shift. Something about doing inventory."

Ricardo swore. "I just did the fucking inventory," he said.

"Yeah, well, I'd do it before log-on. You know how pissy he gets about non-productive time."

Ricardo sighed and got up from the chair. She buzzed him out of the office and shoved her hand into the VR glove. She only had a few minutes before he came back. The Unit Commander had gone home hours ago, she knew, and Ricardo was not one to dally upstairs at the coffee machine.

She practically jumped into the VR environment and was momentarily disoriented when she emerged on the Net. She grabbed Phoenix's file from the open cabinet and buried it in the system trash bin. Then she carefully covered her tracks and backed out.

By the time Ricardo returned, she was logging off. "Perfect timing," she said, trying to hide the edge to her voice. "I just finished my report."

"Any excitement?"

"No. Everybody but the Whitson kid went home. I was just about to release him."

"Bail?"

"No need. The holding period expired."

"I thought the UC wanted to interrogate him."

"No one told me," Madeline said. "I just checked the message board."

Ricardo shrugged. "Less work for me. You want me to bring him up?"

"I'll do it. Go ahead and log on." Ricardo turned away and slid his hand into the glove. He snapped the eyepiece into place and became, for all intents and purposes, oblivious to the real world. Madeline buzzed herself out and went down to get Phoenix.

Coming back upstairs with him, she moved to the other side of the glass with Ricardo who slid an envelope through a small opening. "Please put your palm on the reader to your right," he said. Phoenix complied. "You're free to go, Mr. Whitson. Try to stay out of trouble." When Ricardo looked down to apply his thumbprint to the computer pad acknowledging Phoenix's release, Phoenix looked over his bent head. His eyes met Madeline's for a split second, then she looked away, dismissing him.

Phoenix emptied the pouch on the narrow shelf and put his ID and several thin Credit chips into his pocket. He shoved the pouch back through the opening, turned and was gone. Ricardo said, "Man, they stink when they come up out of the hole. I feel sorry for anyone sitting next to him on the Tube home." He shook his head. "You headed out?"

"Yeah," she said. "I've got some time coming. I put in for a few days R&R."

"Back on Friday, right?"

"Festival? Of course. We're all back by Festival."

"Yeah." Ricardo grunted. "Hate that detail. Too much craziness going on to be sure of what's real and what isn't."

Madeline nodded absently. "Well, I'm going to go up and change. See you in a few days, Ricardo."

He buzzed her out and turned away.

Madeline hurried up the wide stairs leading to the second floor. Only a few other Peacekeepers were in the locker room. Most of the day personnel had already gone down to roll call and those just coming off night shift were not particularly talkative. It had been a gruelling weekend.

After changing out of her uniform, she went into one of the empty offices used for report writing and moments later was on the Net. Carefully, she extracted Phoenix's file from where she'd stashed it. Careful not to leave footprints, she deliberately misfiled it. That done, she logged off and went home.

Out in the bright sunlight, Phoenix squinted. He didn't have very many options. It had been nearly a week since he'd been at work and he wondered whether or not he still had a job. He thought of going back to the warehouse but hesitated. There was a possibility the band was being watched and as much as he appreciated their hospitality, he didn't want to endanger them.

He found an open street vendor and bought some breakfast with a fast-dwindling supply of Credits. Work seemed his best bet, he decided at last and headed across town, hoping someone would have a change of clothes to lend him and that his disappearance had not cost him the job.

❊ ❊ ❊

Alejandro pulled on his bicycle helmet and checked that the package was secure behind him. He put one foot on the pedal and swung his other leg gracefully over the stripped-down bike. A long, lazy arc brought him around and he headed across town with a different kind of Contract. This one was a mover's contract for Gabriel Bell's trucking company. The Studio needed nearly a thousand backup tapes moved to the Armory and Bell's company had been doing it for years.

It was a standard run, but for some reason Alejandro felt nervous. He tried to shake off the feeling as he swerved in and out of early morning traffic on this first Monday in August.

❊ ❊ ❊

Phoenix arrived at the trucking company just after 9:00 a.m. The owner, Gabriel Bell, a middle-aged man with a long history of political action, took one look at Phoenix before pulling him off the floor and into his office. "You okay?" he asked.

Phoenix nodded. He looked into the black man's face, saw worry there and grimaced. "I was arrested on Thursday. Just got out this morning."

"They kept you over."

"I know. I'm just hoping the Net will have records."

"Don't count on it. Got a place to go?"

Phoenix shook his head. "Not until Festival. I'm

THE WHITE BONES OF TRUTH

supposed to meet up with some friends on Friday night. I think everything will work itself out then. But I'm worried about Robert."

Bell nodded. "I'll see what I can do. In the meantime, let's take care of the essentials." He guided Phoenix into a locker room and pulled a set of clean coveralls from a locker. "Here, take a shower. Then come back into my office. I'll scrounge up some food."

"Gabriel ... Thanks," Phoenix said.

Bell clapped his shoulder. "It's what we're here for," he returned and then left Phoenix alone to clean up.

✣ ✣ ✣

"I was about your age, I guess," Bell said as he poured coffee into two chipped mugs. He handed one to Phoenix and sat down at the rickety table opposite the young man. "I was twenty-five the year of the failed coup. No one talks much about it anymore, on either side. A lot of people died. There was so much going on then — the country which had been known as the United States for nearly two-hundred-and-fifty years was coming apart at its regional seams. The South's secession really clinched it, I think. But California ... after the Orange county fiasco it was like a domino effect. All the counties started declaring bankruptcy, the Feds tried to come in and fix the problem. That nasty senator from North Carolina was made president in the '12 elections. And more and more of us were finding ourselves without a job, health care, or even welfare. There was a lot of anger and not much hope."

Phoenix wiped up the last of his reconstituted eggs with a piece of bread. "I wasn't even born then," he said,

shaking his head.

Bell laughed. "It was a very different time. I don't know if it was better or worse honestly. Now there are jobs, but much less political freedom. Then at least we were free to speak our minds without as much fear of recriminations, although there was definitely some. It's always a trade off.

"I guess we all knew something was going to happen. And then suddenly we were in the middle of a riot. Started down at the welfare office in what's now Peacekeeper Central. Spread like wildfire up and down the streets. Took the government offices and then just held on.

"When I was a kid, I remember reading about the protests against the Vietnam war in the 1960s. College campuses. Buildings occupied. Terrorist bombings. No one in Washington wanted to listen then either, and it left this black smear over the whole episode. Like we were too deaf to listen to the conscience of a nation. And after that, there was just apathy. It was like government got too big, and change felt impossible. By the time I was aware enough of the world around me to see what was wrong, people were so worn down, so numbed out by the violence and hatred, so broken by the welfare system and the hand-to-mouth existence that no one had any hope anything would ever change."

"But it did," Phoenix said. "If the riots did nothing else, they reformed the welfare system, got a state-wide jobs program going again."

"And created Contracts. It seems like it's either one extreme or the other. Too much government control or not enough. We don't listen to each other," Bell said leaning toward Phoenix in earnest. "We're all screaming at the top of our lungs about this injustice or that one, but no one's

THE WHITE BONES OF TRUTH

listening." Bell leaned back, suddenly deflated. He crossed his arms over his muscular chest. "It's going to happen again," he said.

"Sooner than you think," Phoenix added quietly.

Bell looked at him. "Why do you say that?" he asked.

"I can feel it. Something's going to happen, Gabriel. And it's going to happen soon." The door to Bell's office opened then and a young woman entered. Her chocolate skin glowed in the morning light and when she smiled, it seemed as though the sun came into the room.

Bell got up and embraced her. "This is my daughter, Tasha," he said to Phoenix. "She's going to fix you up with a disguise."

Tasha drew a plastic box from a woven bag she carried. "Hair dye?" Phoenix asked.

Bell nodded. "Bleach, actually. Didn't you always say you wanted to be a blond?" The two men laughed. "I'll have a new ID card ready for you by the time Tasha's done. You can stay with us until Festival."

"I really appreciate this," Phoenix said, rising.

"You would do the same for me," Bell said.

"Yes," Phoenix agreed. "I would." He grinned at Bell and followed Tasha into the locker room.

Just then there was a knock and the door opened again. Alejandro came into the room. He handed Bell the envelope, waited until Bell signed for it. Bell grinned wolfishly as he read the contents of the package. Then he handed the receipt back to Alejandro with a Credit chip. "Keep the change," he said absently.

"Thanks," Alejandro replied and let himself out.

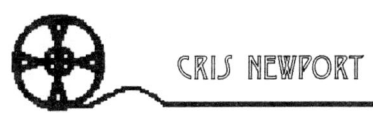

※ ※ ※

The band had been assembled in the practice room for nearly an hour and there was still no sign of Danny-o. Alejandro had already been to the bars in the neighborhood that were Danny-o's favorites, but no one had seen him all day. Now it was getting late and everyone except JayJay was worried. She was simply furious.

"I knew he'd pull some stupid stunt like this," she yelled and flung her drum sticks at the far wall. One stuck into the cork board they'd hung up for soundproofing and vibrated there. The other clattered to the ground.

"I didn't think he'd ever consider leaving the band," Alejandro said. "I guess I misjudged him." He got up from the chair he'd been sitting in and opened the case he stored his bass in. "Well, Kay, it's your turn to play bass." She looked up at him, puzzled. He held the instrument out to her. "I know you've wanted to do this for a while. Now's your chance." He turned to JayJay. "I'll try and cover lead."

"We're not a three-piece—"

"—we are now, JayJay. We've got a gig coming up in five days. A major one. Midnight act on the first night of Festival? It's the chance of a lifetime. And Danny-o or no Danny-o, we've already agreed to perform."

JayJay got up from behind the drumkit and retrieved her sticks. "Well," she said. "I've got a new song. In honor of our first and possibly our last concert. Want to hear it? I figured to make things easier, I'd just set it to a tune we already know: *Valley of Illusions*."

"Go for it," Alejandro said, strapping on Danny-o's guitar. He and Kay tuned up and began the opening riffs.

Downstairs, the rhythmic thumping from the practice

THE WHITE BONES OF TRUTH

room nearly drowned out the sound of the doorbell. Corlay and Michelle exchanged glances, looking up from the laptop which contained the translated e-mail messages JayJay had printed out for them before she'd gone upstairs to practice. Corlay rose and went to the monitor. It was a young woman, a bike messenger. Corlay spoke into the wall mounted microphone, "Can I help you?"

"Got a delivery for Alejandro Jardines or Daniel O'Brien."

"Put it in the drawer."

"You gotta sign for it," she said.

"No problem."

"You one of those guys?"

"Yes," Corlay lied. "Now put the delivery in the box."

The messenger complied and Corlay retrieved the package. She signed Alejandro's name to the receipt and sent it back through with a tip. The girl waved and turned away. Corlay brought the package into the living room and set it down on the table. "It's from Oilslick," Corlay said. "Think we should interrupt them?"

Michelle shook her head. "They just got started. We'll go up when they take a break." She turned her attention back to the small computer screen. Her hand flew suddenly to her mouth and she gasped. "Oh, my God."

"What?" Corlay leaned in for a closer look. The monitor displayed a clipping from the *Times* which had been included in an e-mail message. The headline ran: *Woman Dies in Bondage Scene Gone Bad.* Corlay glanced to the bottom of the page and saw someone had typed after the article: *Everything's taken care of.* Lifting her eyes to the story's beginning, she began reading. *Caroline Wills, thirty-seven, was found dead in her downtown apartment by*

Peacekeepers early Saturday morning, the victim of what appears to be a sexually related crime. Wills was found handcuffed to a door and had been repeatedly raped with a blunt object... Corlay stopped reading.

Michelle was crying soundlessly. Corlay drew her into a tentative embrace. "They didn't have to do that," she sobbed.

"No," Corlay said, and thought, *but it sends an effective message, doesn't it?* Everyone who knew Caroline or knew what had happened to Michelle, which Corlay assumed would be the stuff of deliberate rumor, would know The Studio did not tolerate these kinds of attacks on their property. It both frightened and relieved her and she felt a curious sense of twisted justice. She, too, had wanted Wills dead, or at least punished. But she also knew this was not the way. Vengeance was not justice. Not matter how good it felt.

"What are they going to do to me when they find me?" Michelle asked, genuinely frightened now. "They've got to be looking for me by now."

"No one is going to find you. And as long as I'm around, no one is going to hurt you."

"Corlay, that's sweet, but how can you promise—"

"—I'll do everything I can. That much I can promise you," she said. "Try and forget about it for now, okay?" She drew Michelle closer, wanting to promise more but wondering just how much protection she could offer, wondering what they were going to do with the rest of their lives.

※ ※ ※

Near 10:00 o'clock the band took a break and came

THE WHITE BONES OF TRUTH

downstairs. Corlay and Michelle had separated the messages into two piles. Alejandro came into the room first, massaging his left hand. He shook it out and said, "Been too damn long since I played lead." Then he laughed.

Corlay handed him the envelope from the messenger and he tore it open. He stood reading in silence for a while. JayJay and Kay came into the room. When Alejandro looked up, they were all watching him expectantly. "Well," he began. "They didn't think too much of our changes. It looks like they restored much of the Contract to its original form and made a few concessions. They've agreed to pay us monthly instead of bi-monthly, we get the keep the name of the band the same ..." He scrolled through pages then said, "But almost all the artistic control we asked for has been denied." He threw the com-pad down on the table. JayJay picked it up and began reading through it. "But they've sweetened the deal," he continued, waving a Credit chip in the air. "If we sign before Festival, we get a ten thousand Credit advance."

"Shit," Kay said. "Can I see it? I've never seen so much money before."

Alejandro handed her the chip. JayJay looked up, disgusted. "This isn't at all what we asked for," she said. Alejandro nodded and then sat down beside her on the couch.

"We have some decisions to make," he said. "If we sign now, we already put ourselves ten thousand in the hole. We could stall them a little more but that's a big risk. I don't think we're going to get what we want in any case, but I don't want to lose the opportunity to play on Friday or the payment for that event."

"That's not much of a choice," JayJay said. "So what if we stall them until after the Festival. Where will it leave us?"

Corlay broke in. She turned the laptop toward JayJay and said, "I think it might leave you with a whole new set of options."

JayJay leaned forward. "You found what we needed?"

"I sure as hell did."

"Will someone please explain to me what the hell's going on?" Kay demanded.

JayJay answered, "Of course. It's really quite simple. If we destroy the Contracts, and I mean *all* Contracts and *all* the records of them, then won't we have to begin from scratch? Won't we have to write agreements that are fair to both artist and producer?" Kay nodded, still confused. "Through my incredible talent as a NetSurfer, I've found out two very valuable pieces of information. One is where the backup copies of all the Contracts are stored. And the other," she paused and looked at Corlay, "is the fact someone has created a virus which will wipe out the entire computer system for The Studio. It can, by the way, also be used for Oilslick or any other corporation. Not only that, but the creator of this brilliant virus is also willing to help us.

"My proposition, therefore, is to destroy all the records so The Studio will have no way to prove what the stars owe them. Then the real negotiations can begin."

"But the backup files. Aren't they stored in some old munitions building that's supposedly indestructible? The Armory?" Michelle asked.

"Nothing is indestructible," JayJay said. "Not when you know the right people. And I have just the man to do it. His name is Gabriel Bell. He's the one who blew up the capital building in the coup of '25. He's working at a trucking warehouse downtown."

THE WHITE BONES OF TRUTH

"Are you sure he'll do it?" Corlay asked.

"He'll do it," JayJay said, glancing at Alejandro. "Because I've already asked him."

"So what you're saying is we stall Oilslick until after Festival and at that point we can negotiate a new Contract. Since all their records will be destroyed and their business in a shambles, they might be more inclined to bargain with us," Alejandro said. JayJay nodded.

"But what if it goes completely wrong and we all end up in jail?" Kay asked.

"It's a risk we have to take. At this point, what do we have to lose?"

"Our freedom, for one," Kay said.

"I've been very careful," JayJay said. "This isn't just about us; it's about a lot of people who are fed up with what's going on. I've been NetSurfing for over six months, putting out feelers, seeing who was interested in doing something about the way things are. Everyone who wants to help will be at Festival on Friday night."

"Along with the rest of the population," Kay complained. "I think there are some holes in your plan, JayJay. How are we supposed to know who's there to help and who's just there?"

"About six months ago I found this hidden bulletin board on the Net. Bell and a bunch of other people had already established an organization, a coalition. It was my job to find out where the hard copies were stored. He was going to take care of destroying them.

"Then recently we started getting messages from someone called Deth. This icon claimed to have created a virus which would crash The Studio's computer and destroy all the electronic records. We kept posting notices on the

bulletin board, keeping each other informed. A few days ago, I had the opportunity to meet Deth face to face." She looked over at Corlay. "In fact, she's here right now." JayJay gestured and Corlay nodded her head in acknowledgment.

"You?" Michelle asked, surprise and delight in her voice. "I thought you were a painter."

"I am. But in my electronic incarnation, I'm also Deth. Wreaker of havoc. Hacker extraordinary."

"Do you know Bell?" Kay asked.

JayJay shook her head. "No. I've never met him."

"I have," Alejandro put in. "I deliver there regularly. He's in his forties, I'd guess. Handsome black man. Has an unmistakable voice — soothing or terrifying. I wouldn't want to be on his bad side, that's for sure."

"Phoenix was working for Bell. Might still be for all I know," Corlay put in.

"Have you heard anything yet?" JayJay asked.

"No. Nothing since the other day when I confirmed his arrest. I thought I might try to find out what his status is tonight. See if I can't manipulate the records and get him released if they're still holding him," Corlay said.

"But you still didn't answer my question," Kay said. "How are we going to know who's who?"

"Bell proposed a headband. It's white with a red slash in the front. He says it was the symbol for the failed coup. The blood of the innocents."

"Wow," Kay said. Her brow furrowed thoughtfully. "Cool. So where can we get them?"

"Some second-hand store downtown is one distribution point. The Blue Parrot. I thought you could get them tomorrow, Alejandro, when you're working."

"Sure," he said. "But we still haven't decided what

THE WHITE BONES OF TRUTH

we're going to do about this Contract."

"Can we at least cash in the chip?" Kay asked.

"I'll tell you what," JayJay said. "Let me fax a message to Oilslick telling them we'll sign the Contract on stage after our performance Friday night. Let them make it into a big publicity event. If they let us take the advance now. They'll know we'll be in debt to them. I can't see how they could say no to such great free publicity."

Everyone agreed. JayJay got up and went to the Net terminal. She came back a few minutes later. "They bought it," she said, grinning.

"Well," Alejandro said, "the only thing left for us to figure out is what to do about Danny-o."

※ ※ ※

It was nearly 3:00 a.m. Tuesday morning when Corlay crawled beneath the light blanket beside Michelle. Michelle, feeling the bed shift under Corlay's weight, came up slowly out of sleep. "Hey," she murmured, moving closer, "What time is it?"

"Late," Corlay replied. In the pale orange glow from the city light, her face looked drawn and tired.

"What did you find out?"

"I was on the Net for nearly three hours. Phoenix's record is gone. Simply gone. There aren't any traces either. Someone obviously knows his or her way around," Corlay said, her voice tight with anxiety. "Either he's been killed, is being held without charges or the possibility of bail or he's been released. I'd like to believe the latter, but I can't convince myself one of the former options might not be the truth." Corlay pulled off her street clothes and climbed into

bed beside Michelle in an oversized tee-shirt.

"Oh, Corlay," Michelle said. "I'm sorry. What can we do?"

"Nothing. That's the whole problem. There isn't a damn thing I can do." She sighed and was quiet for a long time. Michelle snuggled tentatively against Corlay's side and Corlay lifted up her arm so Michelle could lay her head on Corlay's shoulder.

Michelle put her arm across Corlay's torso. "Is this okay?" she asked.

"It's nice," Corlay said, her voice rich and warm in the dark. She stroked Michelle's hair with her fingers. "You know, I never imagined my life would turn out like this. That I'd find myself sleeping on a lumpy mattress in an old warehouse on the eve of what might well be the revolution of our generation."

"Our generation? More like the revolution of the century," Michelle put in.

"Maybe. If it works."

"You don't sound hopeful."

"Right now, I feel defeated. I wonder whether someone knows about the virus, traced it to me and is holding Phoenix hostage. I keep going over all my Net encounters, trying to remember if I said anything, betrayed myself somehow. I can't find anything ..." Corlay shifted anxiously.

"There probably isn't anything," Michelle said, tightening her arm in reassurance.

Corlay was silent. "You're probably right. I'm worrying too much because it's so close I can almost touch it. I've waited a long time for this."

"How long?"

THE WHITE BONES OF TRUTH

"About fifteen years. Since I first heard you'd signed a Contract. Even then there were rumors about what Contracts required. You were someone who had shown me decency instead of hatred. That made me want to protect you somehow. Do something to pay you back."

"What I did for you all those years ago never required payback, Corlay," Michelle said. "I never thought you owed me something. I did it because it was the right thing to do, not because I was gathering favors to call in later."

"I know," Corlay said. "It was just something I imposed on myself."

"From such a small moment?" Michelle looked up at her in surprise.

"For you it may have been a small moment. For me it was everything. My life has been lonely, Michelle. I am hated and feared everywhere I go. The few people who even dared approach over the years were often only curious. Drawn to me, but repulsed at the same time. Until very recently my only real friends were other androgynes. Phoenix's friend Robert's father was an androgyne. The four of us lived together for years when the boys were younger."

"Where is he now?"

"Dead. He committed suicide. Many androgynes died by their own hands. We were created by science and then abandoned by our creators. Left to find our own way in a society which found us as horrible as Frankenstein's Monster."

"But you're not horrible. Only physically different. You're not made out of the bones and blood of corpses as the Monster was, but out of human genes."

"But we were engineered. We were the result of what some called Orwellian experiments. We are the product of

humans playing God. Those who made us should have been hated, not us. We were merely victims of the cultural rage at tampering with what some believe belongs only in the hands of some invisible creator."

"Why did they do it? What were they trying to prove?"

Corlay shrugged in the semi-darkness. "The truth has been lost, twisted into a story which bears very little resemblance to the original design," she said. "But at the heart, at the core we were supposed to be the perfect humans. The perfect balance of male and female. Both physically and emotionally. We were supposed to deliver humans from their gender wars. We were supposed to be the beginning of a revolution that would shatter ideas of dominance and submission. Androgynes, because we are both male and female, might have been an example of peaceful coexistence."

"But instead you became the focal point for hatred."

"As anything which falls outside the accepted norm is. We're all different from each other. Unique and special. But we spend so much of our time and energy labelling others, defining ourselves in terms of what we are or are not ... we waste so much of our precious time trying to suppress those who don't fit the picture of who we think we should be. Fearing what is different instead of celebrating it. It's always been this way," Corlay finished quietly. "And I fear it will always be."

"But underneath, you're just like anybody else."

"Yes. And no. My experience as an outsider has changed me. And the very fact my body is both male and female makes my experience of living in it unique. But I am still human. I have a desire for connection, for intimacy, for

love. I have anger and fear and hatred. I am as different from you as I am similar to you."

"I think that's what I most like about you, Corlay. The fact you are so different from me, and yet you're so like me." She moved her hand so it lay palm down on Corlay's stomach, then pushed the material of her shirt aside so her hand rested against Corlay's skin. "You're skin is so smooth. You don't feel like the other men I've known."

"The resemblance is slim, at best."

"It's confusing."

"What is?" Corlay asked.

"Right now, as I lay here with you I feel so certain of myself and of you. I feel safe with you, Corlay. It's been years since I've felt safe with anyone, let alone in someone's bed. I'm attracted to you physically. I guess that's what's confusing."

"We're taught to identify with one gender," Corlay said. "To be attracted to men or women or perhaps both. But not both in one person. You're heterosexual, and while I have physical attributes of a man, I am not male in the way you know men."

Michelle agreed. "And so I find myself wanting you, finding I love the person you are but ... I don't want to hurt you. I'd be devastated if I hurt you, Corlay. You are the most gentle and considerate person I've ever known."

"You must promise me you'll be true to yourself. No matter what. Don't love me out of some desire you have to protect me from hurt. Love me because it feels right. I'd rather have only your friendship and see you with another than have you in my bed knowing you feel confused or uncertain. Promise me."

"I can't," she said, her voice thick with tears. "Don't

ask me to promise something like that."

"Promise," Corlay said again. "Or I will get up right now and walk out of your life forever."

Michelle's arm tightened around Corlay. "No," she said. "You can't do that." Corlay didn't reply. Finally Michelle said, "All right. I promise."

She felt Corlay relax again and a moment later, Corlay's fingertips touched her head. "Turn over," she said. Michelle turned away and felt Corlay shift beside her, felt Corlay's arm wrap around her and pull her close. And encircled, she slept.

Tuesday came and went and Danny-o still did not return. All across Screen City a net was slowly tightening. As preparations were made for Festival, a veritable army of men and women were also preparing, but for a very different kind of celebration.

Gabriel Bell rubbed his palms together and then banged on the back of a truck. He stepped to the side and gave the thumbs-up sign to the driver and watched the vehicle, filled with backup disks bound for The Studio's vault, pull out of the loading area. He grinned wolfishly. Five thousands disks, each wired with plastic explosives.

Phoenix came up beside him, his hands and face grimy from the loading dock. "I heard a rumor your friend Robert is going to be allowed to attend the Festival on Friday night," Bell said, staring straight ahead. "I just happened to mention your favorite hangout place to him and he said he'd meet you there at sundown."

Phoenix threw his arms around Bell. "How'd you do

THE WHITE BONES OF TRUTH

it?"

"Never mind that, boy. Just be there at the appointed hour." And with a chuckle, he departed.

※ ※ ※

"I have good news," Alejandro said, coming through the door on Tuesday night. "Phoenix was released Monday morning."

Corlay sank into a chair, relief flooding her features. "How did you find out?" she asked.

Alejandro smiled. "Did some deliveries to Peacekeeper Central late this afternoon. Some guy named Ricardo was getting chewed out because a prisoner had been released yesterday that the Unit Commander wanted to hold. Ricardo didn't know anything about it. I just sort of hung around for a minute finishing my padwork, you know? Heard Phoenix's name. He's been released and the Unit Commander is pretty pissed."

Corlay sighed. "Thanks, Alejandro," she said. "I was really starting to worry."

He squeezed her shoulder as they sat down at the table together. "No problem." The group sat down to what was, for them, an uncommonly large meal. Kay had cashed the Credit chip and Corlay and Michelle had spent the afternoon with her at the grocery store. It was the first meal they'd had with meat since their last big gig two months ago. After dinner they even had brewed coffee with real cream. It felt like a holiday.

"Any word from Danny-o?" Alejandro asked JayJay as they headed up to the practice room.

JayJay shook her head. "Not a thing," she said. "Not

a thing."

✲ ✲ ✲

By seven p.m. on Friday, August 5th, all the offices were closed up tight. The streets were clogged with pedestrians and all traffic, except for emergency vehicles, had been banned until midnight on Sunday. On a Net terminal buried deep among thousands of secretarial cubbyholes in The Studio's main offices, a screen flashed for a second, then dimmed. An error message crawled across the bottom of the screen in garbled English and inside the vast system, a little virus began to chew its way through data.

At Robert Hennigan's home, the overnight guard came on duty and relieved the man at the central command center they'd established in Hennigan's living room. Thirty minutes after he came on duty, the guard buzzed Hennigan's room. "Message from Central, sir," he said. "You've been granted an evening's pass to Festival."

Robert stared at the screen. "What?" he asked.

"An evening's pass, sir. And I understand there's a particular sausage stand that serves terrific food. Best time to eat is at sundown, sir."

Robert's mind was racing. He looked out the window. Not much time. "Of course," he said. "I'll be leaving in five minutes."

✲ ✲ ✲

Corlay brushed her fingers through Michelle's close cropped hair. "I can't get over how different you look," she said.

THE WHITE BONES OF TRUTH

"I've always wondered what it would be like to try and pass for a man. Just never had the guts to find out. Do you think I look enough like a man to pass?" Michelle asked.

"It's Festival. You'll do fine."

"I don't want to be recognized by anyone from The Studio."

"You won't be. Don't worry. How am I?"

Corlay turned slowly and Michelle admired the man shape. She felt herself flush and then nodded. "Great," she said. "You look great."

They left the warehouse together and headed downtown.

The first band was already on stage when JayJay, Kay and Alejandro arrived. There was a large tent set up behind the playing area, which had been roped off and was patrolled by Peacekeepers instructed to keep all visitors away. The band hung up their performance clothes and stored their instruments in the palm-keyed lockers which had been set aside for them. Then they went to mingle with the crowd and listen to the music.

At the edge of the sunken mosh pit in front of the stage, JayJay scanned the crowd. She could see hundreds of people wearing white headbands with red slashes. It was amazing. Alejandro wore one, too. She looked up at him, watching him watching the band on stage, his body swaying slightly to their music. Kay slumped beside her, eyes vacant. She hadn't said much about Danny-o since he disappeared and it seemed he had taken a big part of her with him.

Dusk fell and the band retreated to the tent to get

ready.

About a half an hour before they were scheduled to perform, there was a disturbance on the perimeter of the fenced-off area. Alejandro stuck his head out of the tent and swore. "What is it?" JayJay asked.

"It's Danny-o," Alejandro replied.

The three band members crowded together on the other side of the rope. Danny-o, clearly drunk, was arguing with one of the Peacekeepers. "But I'm with the band," he kept repeating. "The Bandshees. That's my band."

Another Peacekeeper came over to where the three were standing. "Do you know this man?" she asked. "He claims he's with you. If we let him in, in his condition, you are responsible for him." Alejandro looked at the others. JayJay's face was red with fury. "Do you know him?" the Peacekeeper asked again.

"How could you do this to us?" Kay asked. "We were counting on you." Kay paused and then said more quietly, "I was counting on you."

Danny-o spluttered, trying to make his mouth work. "Just give me another chance," he pleaded, his body reaching out toward hers.

"Fuck that," JayJay spat. Kay turned and glared at her and she fell silent.

"We gave you a lot of chances. Whenever it was important to you, you were there, but if it was important to someone else, you didn't give a shit."

"That's not true," he whined. "There were lots of times—"

Kay cut the air sharply with her hand, silencing him. She looked at the Peacekeeper and said, "He quit last week," she said. "He's no longer with the band."

THE WHITE BONES OF TRUTH

The Peacekeeper turned to Alejandro for confirmation and he nodded mutely. Kay walked away, shoulders hunched against Danny-o's curses. JayJay ran after her, tried to put her arm around Kay's shoulders, but Kay threw it off. JayJay paused, caught between Kay and the violent struggle going on beyond the rope. Two Peacekeepers were trying to get Danny-o to leave quietly, but he would have none of it. Finally, a third came up behind Danny-o and cuffed his hands behind his back. When Danny-o tried to slip out of his grasp, the new officer took out a club and calmly hit Danny-o on the side of the head. He crumpled to the ground and lay still. Two officers picked him up and dragged him away.

JayJay looked at Alejandro. In the crazy Festival lights, his face was unreadable, his posture stiff. Then he turned and his expression softened. He came to her then, took her offered hand. Shaking his head he said, "I never really thought we'd lose him this way. To the drink. Maybe I didn't take it seriously enough. Maybe we didn't try and help enough."

"No," JayJay said. "He made his choice. You can't help a man who doesn't want it."

Alejandro nodded and they went into the tent again.

Earlier that evening at the far edge of the pavilion which had been erected for this event, a large yellow tent flapped in the evening's breeze. Smells of grilled meat and onions wafted overhead in great greasy clouds. Corlay's stomach rumbled and Michelle laughed. "You should have eaten more lunch," she admonished.

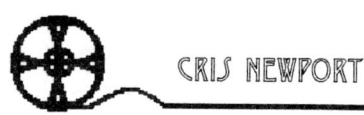

"Um," Corlay agreed without hearing her. Her eyes moved restlessly over the crowd.

A young man came cautiously up to them. "Do you remember me?" he asked. Corlay stared at him for a moment, then shook her head.

"I'm Robert Hennigan." He touched the headband at his forehead nervously. "I got a message to meet someone here. Was it you?"

"Robert? I didn't recognize you," Corlay began, then froze, her eyes focused on something over Robert's shoulder. He turned, following her gaze and then ran toward a young man who looked like a carbon copy of Corlay except for his blond, almost white hair. Beside him stood a handsome black man and a young woman who looked like his daughter.

Corlay hurried to Phoenix, embracing both men at the same time. They all held on as if they had never expected to see each other again. Then Phoenix made the introductions.

Gabriel Bell shook Michelle David's hand and smiled. "I have always admired your work, Ms. David," he said. "And now," he gestured to the headband she wore. "I admire it even more." He turned to Phoenix, Robert and Tasha. "Come on, folks, we have work to do."

"But you only just got here," Corlay protested, her hand reaching for her son. "There's so much—"

"—I'm okay," Phoenix said. He came to her and took her hands in his. "Everything is fine. I was released Monday morning. No torture. No interrogations. I went back to work and have been staying with Gabriel ever since. I was afraid if I contacted you they'd find me or you before tonight. I'm sorry if I worried you."

Corlay squeezed his hands. "I was worried. And I'm sure I'll worry again before the night is out."

THE WHITE BONES OF TRUTH

"I promise I'll be careful," he said. Then, "Tomorrow. Three p.m. You know the place."

Corlay hugged him again. "Be careful," she said into his ear.

"I will. I love you."

"I love you, too." She watched until the crowd swallowed him up and she couldn't see him any more. Then she turned back to Michelle. "Well," she said. "What do you think of my son?"

Michelle grinned. "He's as beautiful and handsome as you are."

❆ ❆ ❆

Street Captain Madeline Mahoney stood on the edge of the crowd. In full gear, she looked imposing and made every effort to heighten the impression. Something was going to happen tonight, she could feel it.

Another Peacekeeper approached her. He took off his helmet and wiped the sweat from the inside of it and then wiped his face. "My air control unit's not working," he said.

She looked at him, knew he could only see his reflection in her visor and that it disconcerted him. "Take yourself out of action and get if fixed," she said crisply. Her head moved back and forth, scanning.

"What's with these headbands?" he asked. "The design looks familiar, but I can't place it."

She looked at him. To be ignorant of history was to be ignorant of the past's impact on the present. She knew exactly where she'd seen those designs before. "Maybe you should look it up," she said.

He scowled and she knew he thought her just another

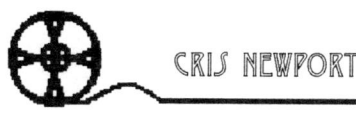

tight-assed Captain. She smiled inside her helmet and fingered the headband stuffed deep into the pocket of her uniform pants.

❉ ❉ ❉

Gabriel Bell was very good at what he knew best. And what he knew best was explosives. Now, standing on the roof of a building half a block from the Armory he was determined to destroy, he felt a certain sense of satisfaction in his work. In his pocket was the detonation device. All he had to do now was wait for the stroke of midnight when the fireworks would begin.

❉ ❉ ❉

Michelle and Corlay wound their way through the crowds. They could feel the tension rising and Corlay, quick to read the temperature of a crowd about to turn into a mob, guided Michelle through a series of alleys which led to a larger open area surrounded by the tall buildings of downtown. "It's getting dangerous," she said. "We should leave now."

"Don't you want to hear JayJay's band?"

"Yes, but it isn't safe here."

"All right," Michelle agreed. "But where should we go?"

"I have an idea," Corlay took Michelle's hand in hers, and led her away from the churning crowd.

It was an older building, but still one of the taller ones. Corlay, using an access card she kept current because of her association with the tenth floor gallery, walked

THE WHITE BONES OF TRUTH

through the lobby toward a series of elevators. The lobby was deserted except for a lone guard who waved at them as they passed by. In the elevator she pressed the button for the roof.

The sky glowed with lights from the surrounding buildings and about fifty storeys below them and a bit north they could see the pavilion. Sound, indistinct and muffled, floated on the evening breeze. Corlay engaged the lock mechanism on the roof patio's door. They walked to the waist-high ledge edging the roof. The patio was furnished with a covered swimming pool, deck chairs, a tended patch of grass and several tables. They stood close together, listening to the sounds of the celebration rise toward them.

Corlay turned to Michelle after a moment and brushed her fingers through Michelle's hair. Michelle closed her eyes and laid her cheek against Corlay's chest. She felt Corlay's heart beating against her skin and the steady rhythm soothed her.

Corlay's ability to hold this male shape intrigued her. She was broader-shouldered and seemed taller, but Michelle knew the latter was an illusion. Corlay had explained the physiological aspects of this to her earlier in the day, how she could control the testosterone levels in her body which, over a period of time, would give her a more masculine appearance or, in the case of sudden surprise or fear, kick in quickly like adrenaline, giving her a rush of added strength.

This latter rush could also be triggered deliberately through a series of techniques involving biofeedback Corlay had mastered in her early twenties. It had been that type of response, coupled with her empathetic desire to please, which had caused the shift Michelle had seen that first night.

But eventually, it would become physically exhausting and, like an adrenaline rush, would subside. Corlay's body would attempt to bring itself back into stasis, into a hormonal equilibrium which would soften her features and stop the slight growth of beard that was not much more than a five-o'clock shadow. It would also bring her voice, already deep for a woman, back into a more normal vocal range.

Looking at Corlay, Michelle had to admit she liked what she saw. Corlay was a masterpiece of engineering — a human who produced both egg and sperm, who had the ability to procreate without the help of another.

It was the person she loved, the entire package she found alluring. It wasn't as much about gender as she'd thought and even though Corlay referred to herself as "she", Michelle thought she was as masculine as some men she'd met and as feminine as some women. She was the best of both genders: strong, sensitive, gentle, confident. Michelle had never met anyone like Corlay and she knew her desire for Corlay's touch was as much physical presence as emotional.

She squeezed Corlay in her embrace and felt Corlay's fingers in her hair. She wanted suddenly to feel Corlay's hands on her skin. She lifted her head, tilted it back slightly and looked into Corlay's dark eyes. "You know," she said, smiling up at Corlay. "You're a bi-sexual's dream."

Corlay blushed then laughed out loud. "Yes," she said. "I guess I am."

"I've been thinking," Michelle said.

"Have you?"

"I want you, Corlay. I want to feel you inside me. Right now. Being with you has reminded me of the person I really am. And I don't want to lose that. I want to know you, Corlay."

"Know me how?"

"As you. As an androgyne. I want to make love with

THE WHITE BONES OF TRUTH

you as you are. Whether you've got more or less testosterone than the average single-sexed person is beside the point."

"Are you sure?" Corlay asked.

Michelle could see the hope on Corlay's face. The hope and the fear of what Michelle would say. "Oh, yes," she said. "I'm sure. I have never been more sure of anything."

Corlay smiled slowly. She closed her eyes for a moment as if in silent prayer. Then she lifted Michelle's face to hers, sought her mouth hungrily. They fell laughing in the grass, fumbling with clothing. Michelle's hands slid beneath the cloth, stroked the smooth skin beneath. She pressed her hands to the front of Corlay's loose pants and felt the familiar hardness of an erection against her palm. With deft fingers, she tugged the drawstring loose and freed Corlay to her touch.

A moan of sheer pleasure escaped Corlay's mouth as Michelle's hand moved. Michelle paused momentarily to slide her own pants from her hips and then she guided Corlay inside her. For one silent moment, Corlay didn't move. She kissed Michelle gently, letting her tongue trace a delicate line along Michelle's bottom lip. Michelle arched up into her and Corlay closed her eyes, her face full of wonder and desire.

"This is ... amazing," Corlay said.

Michelle laughed. "Yes," she said. "It is."

❊ ❊ ❊

It was 11:30. The promoter from Oilslick records was shouting into the microphone but JayJay wasn't paying attention. Her thoughts were focused on the task ahead, on remembering lyrics and music, on the show. Then suddenly there was a roar from the crowd. The band ran on stage and

it had begun.

Just before midnight, JayJay shook the sweat out of her eyes. She signaled Kay, who pounded out the first notes of *Valley of Illusions*, renamed *State of Revolution* for the occasion, and the crowd screamed. They'd scream louder, she thought, when they heard the new lyrics. "Some of you," she said into the microphone, "might know this song. But tonight we've got some new lyrics for you. So pay attention!" Alejandro jumped into the center of the stage, energy crackling around him. Sweat flew from his hair and his hands slid up and down the neck of Danny-o's guitar as if he and the instrument were one. Notes screamed through the speakers, crashed down upon the heads of the audience and when the drums kicked in, Kay began to sing:

> *Through the frosted windows*
> *Through the mist and curtains*
> *Behind closed doors*
> *Out on The Studio's floors*
> *Our lives are bought and*
> *Paid for!*
>
> *Sound room's time spent*
> *With the truth absent*
> *Silver screen lovers*
> *Sold to highest bidders*
> *And Independence is a crime*
> *Is this our time*
> *Or theirs?*
>
> *So we gotta demand it*
> *We gotta own it*
> *They aren't gonna hand it*

THE WHITE BONES OF TRUTH

Over
We need a solution
From the Institution
We need a state of revolution!

The crowd was screaming now, nearly drowning out the band. Somewhere in another part of town, a clock began to strike the midnight hour. And on a rooftop, Gabriel Bell and three young activists got ready for the real show to begin.

And if you're Active
You die violent
If you're a film Star
You lie silent
Freedom is never free
My body belongs to me
What we need now is breath
Silence equals death!

As the band launched into the final chorus, an explosion ripped open the night sky. Chaos erupted in the pavilion as fire shot up like a beacon of change into the darkness.

On a crowded corner, Street Captain Madeline Mahoney raised her hand in triumph. Jerking the helmet from her head, she threw it into the crowd. She tied the headband around her damp hair and threw herself into the fray.

A handful of other officers joined the ranks of the revolution, turning on their brethren, joining the thousands of angry protesters pounding the Peacekeepers, the symbols of the repressive government, into the ground.

In a hundred offices, a virus chewed quietly through bits and bytes of data. And on a rooftop about a half mile away, Corlay lifted her head from where it had been resting on Michelle's chest. Her fingers stroked Michelle's skin. "It's

begun," she said. They rose together, pulling their clothing around them against the damp night chill. Together, from the edge of the rooftop, they watched the city burn.

* * *

As soon as the Armory exploded, the band stopped playing. The raised stage seemed like the only island of refuge in a swirling sea of chaos. JayJay screamed to Alejandro and Kay to get back from the edge of the stage. Sounds of gunfire erupted in the distance and there was the unmistakable smell of tear gas.

JayJay dropped to her knees and began pulling back the carpet covering the stage in front of her drumkit. Alejandro shouted, "What are you doing?"

"Trap door!" She gestured. "Beneath the stage."

He dropped beside her and they pulled the carpet away. There was a steel ring below and the two of them hauled on it. The door came free and light from the storage space below streamed up into their eyes. "Kay!" Alejandro screamed above the rising tumult. "Down!"

She scampered down the ladder, the bass over her shoulder like a longsword. JayJay went next. Alejandro handed her the guitar and her sticks. He pulled the trapdoor toward him and then scooted down the ladder, fitting the door in place behind him.

They were in a square room with a seven foot ceiling. Above them they could hear voices and footfalls. Alejandro gestured to the area below backstage. "Let's go that way. I think there's a tunnel that will take us out from under the pavilion."

"My drumkit," JayJay said, looking up.

THE WHITE BONES OF TRUTH

"Forget about it," Alejandro said. "Let's just get our asses out of here."

※ ※ ※

Michelle and Corlay arrived back at the warehouse a few hours after dawn. Watching the city burn and Peacekeepers in riot gear patrolling the street had occupied much of their time, though not all. They had managed, through some creative bartering, to get an off-duty taxi driver to bring them to the edge of the warehouse district and from there they'd walked.

JayJay, Alejandro and Kay were all asleep in the living room, piled on top of each other like puppies. JayJay extricated herself from the pile when she heard the door open and greeted them with a yawn and a wave as she headed to the bathroom.

Corlay went to the Net terminal for the news. There were a lot of aerial shots of the pavilion, some scenes at Peacekeeper Central where hundreds were being held for processing and some footage from the shell of the Armory building. The records had been completely destroyed. And while Corlay was watching, the newscaster read the latest breaking story in the series of disasters they were claiming had paralyzed Screen City. "This just in. Officials at The Studio confirmed early this morning that a computer virus has destroyed the entire computer records system. Similar reports are coming in from officials at Oilslick Records, one of last night's promoters, and many other companies as well. There is no word yet about when they expect to have the system up and running, but a company spokesman was quoted as saying it should be within the next forty-eight hours—"

"—forty-eight years maybe," Corlay said and Alejandro laughed. He had come up behind Corlay and now stretched and sighed. "It's going to take them days just to figure out what happened," she said.

"Damn, you're good," he said, only half joking.

"She's not the only one," JayJay said, coming up behind Alejandro and encircling him with her arms. Alejandro, Corlay noted with satisfaction, had the grace to blush. "Who's hungry?" JayJay asked and was nearly overwhelmed by a chorus of shouts.

❊ ❊ ❊

The Studio's parking lot was crammed with protesters.

It was a curious mix, one the news cameras couldn't get enough of. Ex-Street Captain Madeline Mahoney now led a group of armed ex-Peacekeepers who encircled the protesters like a safety net. They were surrounded, in turn, by a ring of camera crews who were finally encircled by the city's Peacekeeping force looking decidedly more nervous than usual.

On a hastily erected platform, one of the most well know and respected actors of the decade, David Green, was speaking into a wireless microphone. "... the Contract system is now officially dead. The members of the newly resurrected Screen Artists Guild will not tolerate such bias again. If The Studio wants to make movies, they need to negotiate *real* deals with us and make promises both sides can realistically keep. We need your help. Now is the time of revolution. Of change. Don't be sucked in by promises of fast cash and your name before the title! United we can change this system.

THE WHITE BONES OF TRUTH

Don't let them divide us again." The crowd roared. He turned and faced the blank windows behind him and spoke again. "We know you're in there. We know you can hear us. You want to make movies? Come talk to us! Treat us like the human beings we are. You want profit? Cut us in on the deal!" He raised his fist. Shouts erupted and a thousand voices rose together.

At the edge of the crowd a small group of people gathered. Some were strangers, some were bound by blood, some by new found respect and love. Michelle stood proudly beside Corlay, fingers lightly entwined with hers. Phoenix, his bleached hair blowing in the afternoon wind, was beside his parent, Robert at his side. The three remaining Bandshees stood close together, listening. Even Kay seemed enraptured, caught up in the powerful current of change racing through the crowd.

JayJay turned from Alejandro and walked over to where Corlay stood. "So what are you going to do now?"

Corlay looked at Michelle who shrugged. "I thought I might go back to the Scan 'n' Save Food Warehouse," she said, half-joking and half-serious. She looked at JayJay and continued. "I don't know what I want to do. I'm not sure I want to go back into the industry."

"But it'll all be different."

"Yes," she agreed. "It will. In time. Once, it was all I wanted. But it's not what I want anymore. I guess I just need to see what happens."

"I'm sure they'll make you an offer."

"They probably will. And when and if that happens I'll make up my mind. But right now I'm just enjoying the feeling of freedom."

"Actually," Corlay put in, "I thought I'd take the four

of us on a little vacation. And you? What will you do?"

"WKMA is playing a bootleg version of *State of Revolution*. I expect we'll get some offers," JayJay said proudly. "But I'm not signing anything unless I have the same rights as the boys."

"Good," Corlay said. "That's as it should be."

"You have the best of both worlds," JayJay said. "You can be either."

"No," Corlay said. "Not the best. Mostly it was the worst. It wasn't that I could be either; it was that I was neither. People didn't know what to make of me. Probably still don't."

"Well," JayJay said, "I'm proud to know you." She stuck out her hand and when Corlay returned the gesture, JayJay pulled her in for a hug.

They said their goodbyes then, there on the street. At the edge of a jubilant crowd on the first day after the revolution.

ABOUT THE AUTHOR

Although Cris Newport is best known for her book reviews which have appeared in *Bay Windows*, *The Texas Triangle*, the *Concord Monitor* and *Lambda Book Report*, she is fast becoming a best-selling novelist. Her first book, *Sparks Might Fly* (1994) was released to critical acclaim and quickly became an international commercial success.

Cris teaches writing and literature in New Hampshire where she lives with her partner and a feline companion. *The White Bones Of Truth* is her second novel. Watch for her book *Queen's Champion*, forthcoming in Pride Publications' *From The Muse* series.

PRIDE PUBLICATIONS
bringing light to the shadows
voice to the silence

Pride Publications
Post Office Box 148
Radnor Ohio 43066-0148

Pride Publications was founded in 1989 by a circle of authors and artists. A publishing house dedicated to shedding light on misconceptions, challenging stereotypes and speaking for those not spoken for. A press created for the authors, artists and readers, not just for profit. A company that is not afraid to march ahead, to bring words into print that are not only rich entertainment, but also new visions of our world. Pride's works are revolutionary twists from the norm. Over the years, we have seen many changes but have stayed true to our goals. We continue to offer only the best contracts to our authors, artists and sales partners, and sell only products of the highest quality. We continue to embrace diversity, to take on projects that others find "too wild, too risky, too truthful". At Pride we believe that risk and diversity are part of life. And life, in all its shapes, sizes, colors, beliefs and orientations should be celebrated! We believe in opening eyes.

For more information about Pride Publications or about how you can become a Pride Author, Artist or Sales Partner, write to us.

Pride Publications
Post Office Box 148
Radnor Ohio 43066-0148

SHOW YOUR PRIDE!

Pride Publications offers white tee-shirts featuring our lion-muse logo in black and lavender, as well as full-color Pride art shirts featuring your favorite Pride book cover or interior art.

Available with full-color art: tee-shirts ($15.00), mugs ($15.00), canvas tote bags ($18.00), baseball caps ($18.00).

And in special celebration of the explosive "The White Bones Of Truth", Pride introduces full-color 20 by 30 inch posters of any Pride book cover for only $12.00!

Send check or money order to Pride Publications.
Please specify size (if necessary) and design desired.

MATTERS OF PRIDE

Bookstores: Pride books are available through distributors as well as direct.
** designates forth-coming titles.

BOOKS AND PLAYS

The Redemption of Corporal Nolan Giles. Fiction. Jeane Heimberger Candido. A rich, haunting tale set during the Civil War by a talented writer and Civil War enthusiast.
ISBN 1-886383-14-6 $11.95

Annabel and I. Fantasy. Chris Anne Wolfe. The tale of a love that transcends all time and all categories. Set in the 1980s as well as the 1890s....
ISBN 1-886383-17-0 $10.95

Bitter Thorns. Adult Fairytale. Chris Anne Wolfe. Magical, romantic retelling of Beauty and the Beast with two heroines. *From The Muse* fairytale series, #1.
ISBN 1-886383-12-X $10.95

talking drums. Poetry. Jan Bevilacqua. Lush prose-poetry plus. Love, life, empowerment. Exploring the strength and questions of gender roles in society.
ISBN 1-886383-13-8 $9.95

The White Bones of Truth. Science Fiction. Cris Newport. In a future where film stars are owned by the Studio and independence is illegal, revolution brews.
ISBN 1-886383-15-4 $10.95

***Fall Through the Sky.* Science Fiction. Jennifer DiMarco. Sequel to *Escape to the Wind*, Tyger and gang discover secrets and prepare to face the Patriarchy.
ISBN 1-886383-16-2 $10.95

At The Edge. Play. Jennifer DiMarco. Haunting, humorous. Powerful, empowering. Two women find love and courage in the face of death.

ISBN 1-886383-11-1 $9.95

GAMES

The role-playing games below are brought to you by RAMPANT, Pride's gaming division. Portfolio bound.

Arena Warriors. Battle adventure where you command a fighting team through the challenges of the Great Arena. Play with friends, alone or through a national club!

RAW92-2 $9.00

Jewel Fighters. Build your fortress, create your fighting force. A game of strategy and skill. Infiltrate your opponent's kingdom and steal her or his Jewel while protecting your own!

RJF92-2 $9.00

Kingdoms. For everyone who loves or hates chess. Play on a regular chess board, but each piece has new names, powers and abilities. An age-old tradition made new!

RKI92-2 $9.00

CHILDREN'S BOOKS

The books below are brought to you by Piccolo Pride, Pride's children's book division. Full-color interiors and exteriors.

**The Magical Child.* Carol DiMarco and Connie Wurm. In the days of castles and kings, dragons and things, there lived a little girl named Angela Marie with a very special kind of magic. A gentle fantasy.

ISBN 1-886383-19-7   t.b.a

**Magic's Dream.* The Great Powers — Wind, Earth, Time, Sun, Moon — help make young Magic's dream come true when Magic dreams of humans! But what happens next?

ISBN 1-886383-18-9   t.b.a

To order send check or money order (plus 10% for postage) to:

Pride Publications
Post Office Box 148
Radnor, Ohio 43066-0148

Readers, Remember!

To honor Gay and Lesbian literary excellence, vote in
the 1995 Lambda Literary Awards!
(Before February 1996)

Categories are: fiction, poetry, mystery, biography,
anthology, humor, sci-fi/fantasy, stageplay/drama,
children's, non-fiction studies, and small press book.

Lambda Literary Awards
1625 Connecticut Avenue Northwest
Washington, D.C. 20009-1013
Fax: 202-462-7257

Vote for "The White Bones Of Truth"
in the sci-fi/fantasy and the small press categories.

Your Writers Thank You!